CW00551062

Samarpan is a monk associated with a reputed organization. He teaches ancient and modern scriptures at the university of the organization. His other books in English are *Tiya: A Parrot's Journey Home* and *Param*. He has also published a collection of poetry in Hindi, *Pathik*. He writes regularly in various journals.

Junglezen Sheru

SAMARPAN

PAN BOOKS

First published in the Indian subcontinent 2014 by Pan
an imprint of Pan Macmillan, a division of Macmillan Publishers Limited
Pan Macmillan, 20 New Wharf Road, London N1 9RR
Basingstoke and Oxford
Associated companies throughout the world
www.panmacmillan.com

ISBN 978-93-82616-28-3
Copyright © Samarpan 2014

Illustrations by Ruma Mukherjee

The right of Samarpan to be identified as the author of this work has been
asserted by him in accordance with the Copyright, Designs and Patents Act 1988.

All rights reserved. No part of this publication may be reproduced, stored in or
introduced into a retrieval system, or transmitted, in any form, or by any means
(electronic, mechanical, photocopying, recording or otherwise) without the prior
written permission of the publisher. Any person who does any unauthorized act in
relation to this publication may be liable to criminal prosecution and civil claims
for damages.

1 3 5 7 9 8 6 4 2

This book is sold subject to the condition that it shall not, by way of trade
or otherwise, be lent, re-sold, hired out, or otherwise circulated without the
publisher's prior consent in any form of binding or cover other than that in which
it is published and without a similar condition including this condition being
imposed on the subsequent purchaser.

Typeset by Jojy Philip, New Delhi 110015
Printed and bound in India by Gopsons Papers Ltd

'If you do not allow one to become a lion,
he will become a fox.'
–Swami Vivekananda

To
Srimat Swami Suhitananda ji Maharaj

I

Long Nose, Long Tail

'Ye are the salt of the earth. But if the salt loses its savour, how can it be made salty again? It is no longer good for anything, except to be thrown out and trampled underfoot.'

–Matthew: 5.13

The forest prepared itself for dusk.

Nature's inviolable rhythm had pushed the fireball of the sky to the western horizon. Forest folks hurried to have their last fill before it became too dark and dangerous to move. Birds were singing their melodies of farewell to a glorious day – a day that was like any other day. Fulfilling. Joyful. Expressive. In a few moments, they would all be sucked deep into the womb of silence and sleep. Variety – the signature of life – would now be lost in the oneness of the invisible.

Suddenly, the rhythm of the forest was shattered by a deafening – 'BANG! BANG!' – the sound that silences life. The boom enveloped the forest, filling the startled folks with the ultimate fear. Everything came to a standstill. Activities stopped. Songs went mute. The terrified forest held its breath in anticipation. Who? Where? How many?

'*The king is dead … the king is dead,*' screamed Chital, the deer, and ran wildly through the forest. His legs were fast but his words were faster. In fact, incomprehensible. Even incoherent.

The forest could not believe what they had just heard. Lion, the king, along with his family, had been killed by the poachers. The king's uniqueness in life now lay levelled into the sameness of the dead of the forest – the forest, which was the sustainer in life and shelter in death for millions.

The forest had been accustomed to the lion family's demanding presence and commanding protection for centuries. Over the period, the inevitability of the presence of royalty had settled in the collective consciousness of the forest. But now, it was rattled by the suddenness of this event.

'What is the worth of our life? A mere bullet,' philosophized the goat.

'The brute has been served well,' the bison commented. Despite his sturdy build, the bison had always been afraid of the lion. 'Good riddance,' he added to impart a certain sense of finality.

'I wish he had paid more attention to our tribe,' said the squirrel. He also had been afraid of the lion all his life, but had been too insignificant to be noticed by the king.

More folks. More comments.

The news of the king's death excited Kaak, the crow, the jungle media. His enthusiasm for cawing the trivialities of the forest was inexhaustible. He was like a freelancer who lives for others so that he can survive himself. But his enthusiasm was not shared by all. That day, as on other days, he was accosted by the combative mynah, 'How does it matter to us aerofolks what happens to the earthbound, you noise-polluter? Stop, or else I will narrate your latest deeds to all.'

Despite his busy schedule, Kaak had picked up the wisdom that 'Crowing in freedom is great, but silence during calamity is better'. He shut up.

By then, the news had got its audience. From Kaak, it was picked up by the kingfisher. While diving to catch a fish in the river, the kingfisher uttered the words and missed the fish. That is how the words were picked up by the fishes living in the mighty river that bordered the forest. Across the river lay the world of menfolk, from where poachers came to kill and capture the helpless forest folks.

'What is a king, partner?' one young trout asked his companion.

Before he could get any answer, he and his companion were eaten up by Magar, the crocodile, who was always in wait for the inattentive. He was a vile fellow. Truly vile. Everything about him was abrasive – his skin, acts, words, and even his tears.

'Wait. We seem to be entering a dark cave,' the senior trout commented. Not being accustomed to entering another's belly, he could not distinguish between a cave and a grave. But the other one could not hold his curiosity. He continued with his discussion amidst the darkness that enveloped them more and more.

It was thus that when Magar belched, out came the smell of the trout, and the news that 'the king is dead'.

Magar then swam down the river when he saw Muktak, the elephant, standing still in the river. He had gone to the river for a drink, but had been transfixed after the shot.

The crocodile abhorred Muktak and never missed a chance to needle him. 'Good evening, Mr Big Nose! Your king is dead,' said Magar with satisfaction.

'Hmm,' was the response of the wise to the unholy. Muktak did not really need the information. His ears had already picked up the news and he had been too shocked to react. The crocodile's words, however, brought Muktak back to the present. He hurried out of the river to avoid the meaningless confrontation with the debased. 'Upeksha – ignoring the dirty' was his mantra for peace.

Controlling the external is easy, but restraining the internal is difficult. Muktak avoided Magar, but he could not contain his inner pain.

'Disaster! Disaster!' he rumbled out of habit. Had there been other elephants around, they would have picked up his calls. But his glorious days of company had been ended by the poachers. He now lived a solitary life, doing good to others and musing over the practicalities of life.

'Disaster!' Muktak finally wailed aloud.

'Ah! Even the wise feel pain,' Magar mocked Muktak, and went down the river belching out the news.

Seniority, wisdom, compassion – that was Muktak. He used to say, 'A senior without wisdom is a showpiece, and a wise one without compassion is like an unripe fruit – bad in taste and bad for health.' He was a true well-wisher of the forest folks.

So Muktak was terribly upset when he saw that within days of the lion's death, the arrogance of the illiterate had taken over the forest. The forest had its share of weak, strong, simple, clever, timid, and wicked personalities. The lion had kept this diversity woven in a cohesive whole. With that unifying thread now gone, the strong bullied the weak, the weak insulted the insignificant, and the insignificant cursed their fate.

To stem the rot, Muktak called a meeting of forest elders to elect a new leader.

Not everyone liked the idea. 'Aren't we doing fine? Why complicate matters by electing a leader when we have all the freedom in the world?'

'Freedom comes to the strong,' said Muktak, 'and strength comes to those who have self-respect. But before you respect yourself, you must learn to respect others. Right now, our folks have forgotten the value of respecting others. Without governance, this will result in collective destruction.'

'But O Wise One, every new leader has a new kind of nuisance value. Consider that too.'

'A leader is a necessary evil. He may turn out to be evil, but he also has the potential to infuse strength into the system. I have heard from elders that in earlier times, the menfolk were like us only – animals. Only much weaker. With time, they grew up to become masters of the world. This was possible because of their choice of leadership. They had good leaders who knew where they were leading their charge, and had a clear picture of what they wanted their people to be. Without proper leaders, they would have continued to be a bunch of barbarians, which they still are when left alone.'

'I agree. We never harm them, but they come to kill us. Barbarians!' exclaimed the goat.

The elders agreed to Muktak's proposal. The very next day, there was a great gathering of animals to elect a new leader.

There was no clearing large enough in the forest to hold the gathering, so Muktak uprooted some trees and beat the ground flat to accommodate everyone. The forest folks assembled in large numbers. Even those that ventured out only at dawn, dusk, evening, or night came to rub shoulders with the day animals for the great cause. Most of them were serious, some were curious, and some frivolous.

Muktak had taken the word of oath from all that they were to behave cordially during the meeting. So, the gathering, strange as it was in its composition, caused strain in the food chain and derailed the pecking order. The predator looked at the prey nearby with a salivating tongue; the stalker breathed heavily at the proximity of the quarry; and the mighty wrinkled their nose at the nearness of the commoners.

Magar had also come as an observer and had taken his position under a tree, waiting for the careless.

Many aerofolks had come to watch a new

history unfold in the forest. They were chirping and tweeting vigorously, like curious onlookers, unaffected by the issues.

Surprisingly, Kaak was conspicuous by his absence. 'Where is the media?' the forest folk asked each other. But there was no satisfactory answer.

The proceedings began.

Before anyone could say a word, the squirrel ran up to the podium. 'I propose the name of Muktak for this responsible post.'

This alerted the conspiracy theorists. They concluded that the whole show was rigged by Muktak to his own advantage.

Whispers started circulating.

'Even a sage has an underbelly! How unfortunate!'

'This is the eternal problem of the old. They just won't let go of power, and when not in power, they become sermonizers. That's the way our old tusk is moving up.'

But that was not true. The fact was that the squirrel had been in awe of Muktak's megalithic size for a long time. He had once asked Muktak shyly how one could grow to that size. 'By eating, my little brother' had been Muktak's reply. This had inspired the squirrel to eat the double of what he usually ate. That sent him reeling with a nasty stomach pain. Since then, his admiration for Muktak had become unflinching; he had suffered doing what Muktak could do effortlessly.

Before the squirrel's proposal could be taken up, a monkey got up to address the crowd. This alarmed many. They knew that if the simian was up, he must be up to some mischief.

'Friends, wait a minute. You really want to make the "long nose" the leader of the forest? Wah! But tell me who among us has a long nose? No one. Why? Because a long nose is an aberration.'

The crowd was struck to silence. *Uniqueness was an aberration?* 'And look, on the other hand,' said the monkey, 'don't all of us have tails? It means that our leader's tail must be of a dignified length. Even the lion, bless his soul, had a long tail. For your information, long nose is the failed line of evolution, whereas long tail is the favoured side of evolution.'

Deafening silence.

'Conclude not that I want power. But we have someone great amongst us. I present before you a new arrival in our community from the city. So far, it has been our poor luck to lose our brothers to the greedy from the city. But this is the first time that we have someone from the city amidst us. Kapi! Our new member. Fresh from the city! Escaped from the dirt! Make him our leader, brothers. You will never regret. Give him a big hand!'

The crowd, eternally stupid as it is, went into frenzied clapping.

The loss of attention of the crowd prompted Magar to inch towards the goat, but Muktak saw the move and sternly asked the predator to leave.

'I will get back at you. There are many scores to settle,' threatened Magar and left.

Kapi walked towards the podium with a sense of purpose. He had worked in a circus for a long time where he had been trained to face the crowd. From there, he had been transferred to a zoo by some animal activists, whom he still freely cursed. In the circus, he was a performer with a group, but at the zoo he had to master the art of solo performance to get extra nuts and fruits from the onlookers.

Being fickle, he had somehow escaped from the zoo. But he regretted it. He was accustomed to good food and being taken care of both at the circus and at the zoo. But here in the forest, he had to eat wild fruits and take shelter amidst trees. Also, he was not high on the pecking order in his tribe. All this had disillusioned him from the great idea of freedom, and he now longed to go back to slavery.

He had been thinking of crossing the river to try a different future when this gathering was called. This filled him with hopes of novelty and prospects – the twin motivation for success. He stayed back.

Kapi reached the stage and stood there in purposeful silence. After a moment, he turned his head, once in this and then in that direction. A plastic smile and a slow movement of his hands sent the crowd into raptures. The circus and the zoo had trained him well.

'What luck to have someone cultured amidst us rustics!' said the goat. Neither he, nor anyone else in the crowd had seen such performance.

Bhalu, the bear, was sitting somewhere at the back. When he had heard about Kapi coming from the city, he had been eager to enquire about the fate of his two brothers who had been captured by the city folks some time ago. Kaak, a regular city visitor, had informed him that the duo now danced in the streets to the beats of a performer. Bhalu had refused to believe that such ignominy had befallen his brothers. But now, he had the prospect of getting some real news about his brothers.

Bhalu moved through the crowd to reach the stage. But that was mistaken as an attempt-to-assault by many. This resulted in fight, fright and flight. To check the stampede, Muktak had to intervene. He brought order by trumpeting and stomping his feet and asked Bhalu to go back to his old place.

The distraction took away a lot of Kapi's airs, but he gathered himself a second time and began, 'Friends, folks, foresters! I stand before you as one of you, although once removed. I consider it my privilege to address you ...'

He then rolled out the achievements and the glories of the animals. To add zing to his words, he freely used sense, common sense and nonsense. A moment ago, he himself would not have believed what he was saying but being a performer, he knew that the art of deceiving and convincing begins with oneself. He was now fully convinced of what he was delivering.

The folks listened spellbound. They did not know that such greatness surrounded them. For the first time in their lives, they felt important.

Kapi was almost at the end of his talk. 'The city folks are the future of the universe,' he said, 'but even there you do not see a long nose. And you will be proud to know that even their kings put on a long tail to imitate our tails!'

The applause was thunderous.

'I also feel proud to inform you that a large number of city folks worship Hanuman, who has a long tail. So my dear friends, folks, foresters! How can you be burdened by a long nose? Down with long nose! Up with long tails!'

Muktak felt sad to be humiliated like this. He did not want fame, but nor did he want shame. However, being the saint that he was, he overcame his emotions and stood tall once again.

The forest now shouted in unison to make Kapi the head of the forest.

To honour their new leader, Muktak broke a branch of flowers and moved towards Kapi. Suddenly, there was a pandemonium in the crowd. Everyone was distracted by the excited crowing of a tired-looking Kaak. 'Yes, the media is here with some big, breaking news.' He was flapping his wings furiously to reach the centre of the gathering.

There is a cub! There is a cub!' he was blabbering.

Surprise.

Silence.

Confusion.

Commotion.

The jumbled expression of Kaak was difficult to decipher, but when they saw a lion cub whimpering and tottering towards them, the meaning was clear.

'A cub! A lion's cub!' The crowd resonated. Everyone ran for his dear life. The power of the lion was embedded deep in the minds of all. Even the aerofolks expressed their excitement through screams and screeches.

Kapi and the other monkeys dropped their ambition to govern the masses and took the tree-route to safety.

The jackals, who had plans of their own for sharing power, ran in vain for the tunnel route. While levelling the ground, Muktak had unknowingly destroyed their underground paths. They now cursed him freely and darted with others blindly.

Like a poor man's fortune, the ground now stood empty.

Muktak trumpeted with joy, threw the flower branch to the ground, rushed to greet the cub, lifted him by his trunk, and then put him down tenderly.

The cub whimpered with fright at all this attention. He had somehow escaped the cruelty of the poachers, and had been starving since the death of his family members. Hunger had made

him come out of hiding when he was spotted by
Kaak, who coaxed him to come for the meeting.

'Lion! Lion! Sheru! Sheru! You are the king!'
Muktak trumpeted.

Sheru, the lion cub, meowed in fright.

No one in the forest wanted to adopt Sheru, so
Muktak took charge of him.

Love is the space in which one finds the freedom
to fly. It is in this space that one's personality is
shaped. A child first finds that space in his mother's
love. With age, he finds that space in his father,
teacher, friends, and family – in that order.

Sheru had none of these, and he had no
possibility of ever having one. Muktak knew this
well. So, to fill the void, he made efforts to be
everything to Sheru. But Sheru had his own ideas
of freedom and growth.

'You see that tree in the distance? Now run up
to that and be back before I finish counting up to
ten,' commanded Muktak.

Sheru looked warily at the distant tree and
decided that he didn't want to do the trip even
if Muktak counted up to a thousand. He quickly
worked out a way to apply his 'won't power' to
counter the willpower of his mentor.

'Yes, Master. Right away. Let us start.'

'Don't be silly, you are a lion. I cannot keep pace with you. Stop offering excuses and run.'

'No way, Master. I will die if I am away from you even for a moment. So either we run together, or we do not run at all.'

Muktak then tried to frighten Sheru by swaying his trunk, but Sheru clung to it lovingly and said, 'This is so comforting. How sweet you are!'

This became a daily ritual.

Muktak resigned his efforts to destiny and wondered what would happen if there was an attack on the forest.

Not everyone in the forest was happy about Sheru being under Muktak's care. Kapi, along with his band of monkeys, sulked at the lost prospect. The jackals too were disappointed. They had wanted to be the power brokers of the new regime, but that prospect seemed bleak now.

Magar had neither forgiven nor forgotten the slight from Muktak. He now plotted his downfall. Magar bribed the jackals with premium fishes, tempted the monkeys with future leadership, and gave them plans to work on. The first step of it was to call a second meeting.

Rig, the leader of the jackals, and Kapi approached Muktak to call a second meeting, but Muktak outrightly refused to do so. 'Monkeying with the leadership will make a monkey of everyone. Sheru is the leader. No discussion on the issue.'

Kapi tried to convince him in the name of cultural progress, and Rig cajoled him with the prospects of economic progress. Muktak replied, 'Sheru is the essence of the forest. The forest cannot be without him. Lost essence is lost competence. Do not even think of fiddling with this.'

The dejected group then went into a hurried whisper and came up with a daring plan. The jackals, heavy with more fish from Magar, got down to lightning action. Inspired by their ideal, fired by zeal, and sustained by hope, the jackals worked the way only the greedy can work. They were cheered in their effort by the monkeys, and soon they were prepared to execute their plan.

The group now waited in certainty for Muktak to fall into their trap, which he did. He was taking his customary walk with Sheru and explaining things to him.

'You are Sheru. You are a lion.'

'I am Sheru. I am lion.' Sheru imitated.

'Oh no! You are not lion. You are ... *a* ... lion. The king. Lion is not your name.'

Before Sheru could reply, both of them fell headlong into a ditch that had been dug by the jackals and cleverly camouflaged.

Muktak trumpeted angrily from the depth of the ditch. Sheru cried.

'Shut up! Do not whimper. You are a lion. Roar.'

'Roar? I only feel like crying. How will we ever get out of this black hole, sir?'

Seeing that the argument had no future, Muktak became silent.

Soon Kapi came to the rim of the ditch and said, 'Mr Muktak, will you be with us or against us? Be prepared to starve for a long time if you decide to go against us.'

Muktak trumpeted in anger. The monkeys shrunk back in mock fear.

'I do not want to die in this black hole, sir. Please. Let us be with them,' whined Sheru.

Saddled with the responsibility of a dependant, Muktak agreed to compromise. He promised to work unconditionally with the monkeys.

That is how, finally, the second meeting of the forest was called.

Cajoled by the clever, the second assembly accepted the leadership of the monkeys. The forest now moved towards a different future. History, traditions, lore, and wisdom were all going to get a new twist.

'We had always been democratic till the lion took over.'

'Magar has always been our well-wisher.'

'Monarchy is a failed experiment.'

Many heads, one view – acceptance of the change.

In his first address to the animals as the leader, Kapi thanked everyone for reposing their trust in him, and said, 'I will always be your humble servant, brothers.'

'The rascal is neither humble, nor a servant, not even a brother. I wonder what will happen to my motherland now,' Muktak rumbled. Sheru looked at him quizzically, but could not understand his silent words.

Kapi announced that he would be advised by a council comprising the leaders of different tribes. Only Muktak and Sheru were left out permanently because there was no one they could represent.

Amongst the jackals, Rig was elected the leader. It was said that he could rig anything out of anything, hence the name. Rig was declared the minister of internal affairs, but his critics claimed that he was actually going to be the minister of sinister aims.

Rig was on the land what Magar was in the river. Wily. He was a master at making a kill of the unguarded, and, like any other weak fellow, he was ambitious. When the lion was alive, Rig always walked behind him in the hope of getting some leftovers. Now with Kapi as the leader, he could allow his ambition to take a free flight.

When the meeting ended, Muktak walked back with Sheru and sighed, 'Lord save the land where a monkey is the leader, and a jackal is the deputy. The fickle and the clever can only ruin the system.'

'And how were things in earlier times?' challenged Sheru. He loved his master, but he saw no reason to be upset at the changes taking place around him.

'The clever and the cunning are weak by nature. So your father never associated with them, nor did he ever keep second-grade deputies. Once you compromise the top, the bottom is automatically compromised.'

'My father, ah!'

Muktak continued, 'Not everything is meant for everyone, Sheru. Destiny fixes something, and then Mother Nature works it out through us. A fruit always falls to the ground but smoke rises to the sky. Everything ultimately finds its right place. In the same way, we too have our fixed place in life. When we force ourselves into a different orbit, the laws of nature take over, and we are once again forced to be what we were supposed to be. During the period that one occupies the wrong position, there is only suffering all around.'

'That is why I never make an effort.'

Muktak ignored the wisecrack and said, 'Would you like to hear a story?'

'Anytime, Master. I love stories. They are more interesting than your instructions.'

'A long time ago, there was a rock that had made its home on a sea beach. All around him lay sand, vast in number but insignificant. This made the rock conceited and boastful. He never let go of a chance to ridicule the small.

'Once there was a big storm, and a lot of sand fell into the ocean. One of those tiny grains got embedded in the body of an oyster. To avoid the irritation, the oyster enamelled it with care. Soon the near invisible grain of sand was transformed into a precious pearl.

'It was now the turn of the sand to laugh at the rock. This angered the rock. He screamed that if the teeny-weeny could become so precious, then he could too, and many times over. And so, after he finished boasting, he rolled into the ocean in the hope of becoming a mega pearl.

'Centuries have passed. The rock continues to lie at the bottom of the ocean, without a ray of hope to escape from his watery grave.'

Muktak concluded his story and asked Sheru, 'I hope you got the idea?'

'Yes, Master. One should not have a large size like you. See how wonderfully slim I look!'

Bhalu became an addition to Kapi's hangers-on. From the days of the first gathering, Bhalu had been eager to have a word with Kapi to find out the truth about his missing brothers. Kapi had no idea about Bhalu's brothers, but he did not want to lose a potential ally for a simple thing like a lie.

'Oh yes,' Kapi told Bhalu, 'I knew them well. It is true that they were captured by the poachers, but now they are living a very good life in a garden which is like this forest. The owner of the garden is a kind person who takes good care of the two.'

Bhalu was overwhelmed. He shed tears of relief and held Kapi in his arms. 'Brother, I will be your slave for life. You have not only saved me from great mental distress, but you have also given me immense joy. Indeed, you alone deserve to be our leader. I promise to serve you all my life.'

Kapi could not congratulate himself enough for his master move. 'Yes, you will serve me with your life,' concluded Kapi, and made Bhalu the minister of security. True to his word, Bhalu carried out every order of his master without ever considering whether it was proper or not.

The news that Kapi had brought joy in the life of Bhalu, spread wide. The innocent came to the conclusion that their new leader had solutions to all their problems. This made the needy throng his durbar regularly. The first to come were the rats. They approached Kapi to change their names.

'Honourable, Mr Leader sir! We get hunted because of our size, and get haunted by our names. The forest folks kill us for their meals, and use our name to insult others. In the old regime, no one paid attention to our plight. But now we see hope. After all, we were also instrumental in your becoming the leader.'

Still fresh in power, Kapi was ready to listen to all, and oblige all. He thought for a moment and then issued orders to change their names to 'rodents'. Anyone found using the old name was to be prosecuted.

However, this change in name did not help matters. Now that they had come in the news, the rats faced even more attacks. So they approached their leader once again for a new name. This time, they were named 'mice'. But things became worse. The teasing and the attacks increased. The elders of mice tribe then approached Kapi again with the same request.

This time Kapi got angry. 'Why do you need to change your names? Only those who are into performing arts take up new names to enhance their marketability. You are not performers. What markets do you want to capture for yourself that you must have a new name?'

'Sir, a new way of life sometimes demands a new name. We appeal that something be done for us.'

That set Kapi thinking. 'New way of life', 'new name', 'changes' – yes. Something drastic had to be done. The fickleness of a monkey brain has its own advantage. It can come up with links between things which others won't even dream of linking.

Kapi had been in the city for a long time. There, despite his frivolities, he had picked up a few tricks of the humans without understanding them. He now got down to implementing the ideas transplanted from the city.

He called his council, placed before them his ideas, suggested to them a new constitution, and declared:

* We are all junglezens
* Good of all, growth of all – is our motto
* Collective over individual – is our way

Kapi called the great gathering of the forest to announce the new dispensation. By then, he had started enjoying his performances before huge crowds, so he never let go of a chance to address them.

'Friends! From today you are no more a rat, cat, bear, bull – or any such silly being. You are all Junglezens. Jai Junglezen!' And he rattled away the new constitution.

The crowd, not accustomed to seeing so many changes taking place so rapidly, shouted in excitement, 'Jai Junglezen!' They loved antics, and so they loved to hear and see their leader perform.

Muktak was aghast with this development. But the last point of the new constitution left him numb. He got up to oppose it.

'Mr Leader sir! Individuality is the sign of life. Collectivity brings good only to those who are going down in life. A snowball rolling down a mountain or a river going down grows in collectivity. But every drop of water has to purify itself to rise high. I request you to delete the last amendment in the interest of individual growth. That has been our way of life. Please do not tinker with it.'

For Kapi, being opposed in public, was worse than having to face Yamaraja, the god of death. He breathed hard and retorted, 'The days of decadent wisdom are gone, Mr Long Nose. You and your wisdom are mere fossils now. Make way for the future. Unity, unity, unity! Unity is the sign of culture. It is the sign of the strong.'

'Culture, my broken tusk! The truly cultured are strong, and the strong never crave company. Desire for collectivity is a sign of weakness and degradation. More degraded an ideal, more followers it has, as you can see in any *tamasha*. There never really was any equality among the living, and there will never be. Inequality is the first law of life. Anyone who talks of equality is a pucca charlatan.'

Seeing that the situation was spiralling out of control, Rig soothed Muktak and reminded him of his promise of cooperation. That silenced Muktak into an angry rumble, 'I wish I had died that day in the pit. I would have been saved of watching the slow dance of destruction.'

'Jai Junglezen!' shouted the monkeys.

The earth and the sky were filled with the shouts of 'Jai Junglezen!'

Sheru was too young to understand the complexities of existence. But like any young person, he loved to be in the midst of the continuous flux that surrounded him. The idea of junglezen excited him tremendously. He shouted, 'Jai Junglezen!', and vowed to stay true to the new concept all his life. 'What is the worth of a life if it is not built on a great ideal?'

Muktak shook his head in frustration. But there was nothing that he could do to stop this circus. He also wondered if he would be able to draw Sheru away from this theatre of the absurd.

'What a decisive moment for all!' Sheru exulted.

'Stupid!' sighed Muktak.

'Why stupid? We, the young, need revolutions every day.'

'With a monkey in power, lions are bound to talk of everyday revolution.'

'There are no more lions and elephants in the forest, sir. There are only Junglezens. Jai Junglezen!'

Muktak was too worried about the safety of his beloved forest to pay attention to the wild enthusiasm of the cub.

Muktak's fears proved correct. The first calamity was already brewing silently.

The monkeys and the jackals organized a coming-to-power celebration, in which Magar, the crocodile, was the chief guest. After the fruits and fishes had been downed, Magar called Kapi and Rig for a closed-door conference.

'Crown comes for a price. What is your take on it?' asked Magar.

'Indeed, that is true, O noble one!' The greedy duo saw an angel in Magar, the Terrible.

'He who gets you into power, can also get you out of it. Say what?' Like any other devious being, he could swim around the point to corner the opponent.

'Yes. We will be caring towards the Junglezens.'

'Junglezens! Pooh! You are acting smart

by suggesting that a crowd of dirty, illiterate bumpkins got you into power. What is a crowd? It is wisdom-blind, and reason-deaf. They only know how to be led, believing all the time that they are leading. So forget all that dirt. I made you what you are today, and I can get you torn and thumped tomorrow if I want.'

Crooks are weaklings who crave power over everything. Rig replied, 'We were joking, sir. You are our only ally. We are the glove and you are the hand.'

'Then do something for your friend! With all the pollutants of the city getting dumped in our nice river, I am getting a nasty indigestion these days.'

'Sir?'

'The fishes in the river are getting polluted. They are no longer good for someone of a delicate constitution like mine.'

'Sir, we have a doctor amongst us. Should we get some herbs for you?' asked Kapi.

'No need for that. Like venom and anti-venom, the cause of the ailment alone can be its cure.'

'Sir, what can we do to make your cheeks rosy?'

'I need a change in my diet. You can help me by sending one animal every day as my curative meal.'

The demand shook both the fickle and the cunning. True, they desired power, but they were not confirmed killers. At least, not yet. But what other option did they have now? So, Rig nodded his head in agreement.

From that day onwards, an animal was singled out by Rig, and was asked to deliver a confidential message to Magar. In turn, Magar kept the secrecy of the message safe by putting the messenger in the safety of his belly.

Occasionally, some bereaved family raised the issue of the missing member, and shed tears. But who cares for lonely tears when the land is teeming with population? The tears, along with the secret of the missing, were to remain buried for some time.

The second attack came from across the mountains.

II

The Donkey School

The forest was surrounded by hills on its three sides. Beyond the mountains lay the kingdom of the cruel. Despite their ferocity, they never dared to attack the forest when the lion was alive.

The wolves were one of the most ferocious tribes, who had tried to invade the forest many times in the past. But the roar of the lion had terrified them into beating a hasty retreat every time. So, they were pleasantly surprised when they heard Magar belch, 'The king is dead.' They decided to investigate, and four daring wolves were sent to the forest.

On reaching there, the gang of four cautiously approached a lonely jackal, 'Ahem! We be of same blood!'

This jackal was neither good with his intelligence, nor with his speech. This had made him an outsider in his own land. Because of his limited speech, no one cared for him, and his limited intelligence did not allow him to struggle for more. 'Maybe,' the jackal was afraid, but non-committal.

Gifts changed hands, and the jackal's speech was lubricated. Yes, the king had been dead for some time. No, there was no new king. Yes, a monkey was the head. No, there were no animals in the forest; there were only Junglezens.

The loner then said, 'Brothers, since you claim to be of my blood, I request you to act on my behalf, and ask my folks not to neglect me.' He then started a long discourse on the evils of negligence and its effects on the sufferer and perpetrators.

The wolves were young and had no patience for the lamentations of the old. They politely promised to hear him some other time, and then galloped back.

Within a few days, the wolf army's war cry rang through the forest.

'Attack! Attack!' screamed the forest.

Kapi was dumbfounded. Being from the city, he was accustomed to performance and clapping. He had no idea about the deadly face of leadership. Also, he was not a leader who knew how to take the low along with the high. To him, leadership was all about power, adulation, and enjoyment. He now cursed his fate.

He was wondering what to do when an idea struck him. He immediately perched himself on a high tree and started screaming, 'To war! To war!' Other apes followed Kapi, and soon all the monkeys were in the safety of height, from where they freely served encouragement.

The jackals howled and howled that wolves, their brethren, could never attack them, and that it was all the ploy of the wicked zens to malign the noble race. They concluded by saying, 'But we are noble zens, so as a compromise, we agree to cheer our army from our tunnels.'

The squirrels agreed to drop nuts from the tree-tops for the fighters, and the goats philosophized on death.

Only Dholu, the donkey, refused to believe that there was anything called 'attack'.

Stubbornness, the eternal companion of stupidity, was Dholu's uniqueness. This made him lose friends faster than he acquired them. If anyone ever hinted at his donkeyness, he retorted with 'the cultured are consistent'. Also, to convince his listeners, he never hesitated to use a hind kick.

When Sheru had been found, Dholu had refused to accept the existence of Sheru. 'Tell me friends, how can there be a cub when there is no lion?' he would ask anyone who was dumb enough to listen to him.

'Why? If you die, will your kids cease to exist?'

'I exist, so my world exists. Where is the contradiction?'

The argument would continue till it was concluded with the hind kick from Dholu to register his final victory over the foolish.

The day on which the wolves attacked, Dholu began, 'Tell me friends, when we are not fighting, how can someone fight with us?' But the forest was too preoccupied that day to argue with him.

Some of the sensible forest folks ran to Muktak for protection from certain death. When he heard what Kapi and Rig were doing, he was shocked. 'Not everyone realizes that pulling is easier than pushing. A true leader pulls everyone forward, but a failed commander always pushes from behind. I am not surprised that Mr Leader has chosen to cheer from a treetop.'

He then agreed to go face the wolf-army. Many animals, who still had a vestige of courage left from the days of the lion, joined him. He then forced a reluctant Sheru to walk by his side to the battlefield.

'Do you think I will be killed, sir?' whimpered Sheru.

'That would be a good idea.'

'Why don't we go to the place where Mr Leader

is perched? We too can encourage the fighters from there.'

'Enough. Now shut up and watch. Incompetence will show.'

'Whose? Mine?'

Muktak decided not to reply. 'Be silent to make others silent' used to be his advice to the quarrelling couples of the forest. He did the same now.

When the forest army reached a clearing, Muktak stopped and took up an aggressive stance. He raised his head and trunk, extended his large ears, trumpeted loudly and started kicking up clouds of dust. Anyone who knew him would have known that it was only an aggressive stance to frighten his enemies. He had no intention of risking a fight and causing mayhem all around. At least not yet. If the wolves had any sense, they would retreat upon seeing the frightening posture of the elephant.

When the leader of the wolves heard the trumpeting of Muktak, he got worried. He ran to a vantage position to take stock of the situation. What he saw, horrified him. There was a lion cub standing by the side of the majestic elephant. An absolute nightmare. The nervous commander called an urgent war council, 'We were told that there is no lion. From where has this one sprung up then? Get the scouts hanged.'

'He is only a cub!' exclaimed someone.

'It is a trap. No cub will fight unless his parents are behind him. We are done for. Should we go forward?' asked the commander.

'What! Attack a lion? The gift of life is better than a few extra morsels.'

By then, the dust had settled a bit, and the wolf-army had got a reality check. When they saw the elephant with the cub, they were first surprised and then terrified. 'Run for your lives!' cried the wolves, and bounded towards the safety of their land.

Fear of death is the ultimate emotion in the living. It makes one run, it also makes one freeze; it makes one talk, it also makes one mute; but it never leaves anyone in doubt. After all, the desire to survive is common to every living being.

The commander tried to bring some order, but he had little chance as his army flew on wings of terror and cowardice.

It was at this moment that Dholu decided to investigate the matter of the junglezens moving in a body, without paying heed to his momentous queries. He ran to catch up with them, but before he could bring himself to a stop, he overshot Muktak, who was leading his army.

By the time Dholu brought himself to a stop, he was face to face with death in the form of the commander of the wolves. He stood alone with his back to his fleeing army. A valiant commander that he was, he did not want to see the cowardice of those whom he led.

The force of conviction of certain death was so powerful for Dholu that, for a change, he did not question whether or not there was a thing called death. That was the first time in his life that he accepted something without questioning its correctness. He turned around to gallop towards his own folks, but in the hurry of his nervous excitement, he chanced to throw his hind legs on the commander.

The wolf commander was already shocked at what had happened, and he was definitely not prepared for a nasty hind kick from a donkey. The poor fellow fell unconscious.

Dholu's lack of wit, and absence of courage, achieved for him what he could have never achieved with all the wit and courage he could hope to collect during his entire life. Yes, karma was surely in a mischievous mood.

Kaak had arrived on the scene just when Dholu had kicked the commander unconscious. He had been busy in the city, and on hearing about the great war taking place in his own land, he had hurried back. What he saw, excited him. He cawed out loudly, 'Dholu won the war.'

Unconcerned by the news, Muktak advanced towards the prostrate commander, lifted him, and threw his inert body over the fleeing army. The wolf came back to consciousness by the force of fresh air and now led his army in flight.

'Dholu won the war,' Kaak crowed and crowed. It was a wonder that his excitement did not kill him.

The jungle echoed the news. Dholu felt humility welling up from within.

The most manifest desire of the living is to be the winner. That is why no one wants to lose even in a simple quarrel, and is on a high even after the most trivial victory. Every other emotion is a mere echo, or at the best, an extension of this desire.

The forest was no exception to this fundamental emotion. The joy of victory exhilarated every junglezen, and when the victory rally was called, the rush among them to be in the front was great.

'Victory is claimed by the crowd, but failure belongs to the leader,' Muktak told Sheru. Muktak was too deep to demand credit for discharging a sacred responsibility, so he stood at the back.

'That is why I never want to lead,' Sheru said happily. He was mastering the art of interpreting the words of his master to his advantage.

Kapi and Rig stood on the podium with a satisfied smile.

'Jai Junglezen!' Kapi greeted. He thanked everyone, reminded them to be vigilant in future too. And he concluded by saying, 'In appreciation of Dholu's services, the council makes him the captain of education for the young zens.'

There were surprised *oohs*, and subdued laughter from the crowd.

Muktak objected to the proposal, 'Mr Leader sir! The responsibility of educating the young lies exclusively with the family. Why do we need to change it?'

'You have no kids, and so there is no reason for you to discuss what does not concern you.'

No use talking to usurpers, Muktak concluded.

Muktak's silence gave Kapi an idea.

'Zens! As a token of Muktak's services during the war with the wolves, the council wishes to honour him in a grand way.'

The forest folks were curious.

'Muktak will have the privilege of carrying Mr

Leader, that is me, on his back. Give him a big hand, junglezens!'

The crowd went into a state of stupid surprise.

Kaak had been sitting on the branch above the podium to get maximum coverage. On hearing the proposal, he became excited and pooped on Kapi's head. The yellow head of the monkey was dotted white.

Kapi screamed, 'This black deed of Kaak is the well hatched plan of the reactionaries. The beastly bird is on the payroll of the enemy who are jealous of our progress. I order you all to destroy the outrageous.'

Kaak had wanted to apologize to Kapi for his nervous act, but the outburst of arrogance annoyed him. When the monkeys jumped up the tree to punish Kaak, he flew away, and heaped some choice abuses on the monkey business. His trips to the city had increased his vocabulary substantially.

The story goes that the crows and monkeys have been at war since then.

Barak, the goat, saved the situation. He bleated loudly, 'Friends, leave Kaak alone. I assure you that this white mark on Mr Leader is a sign from the Divine to carry on with our noble work. Onward, junglezens!'

The forest folks looked dumbly at each other. Sheru whispered to Muktak, 'Poop as divine signal! How exciting.'

'Learn to be silent if you cannot talk sense.'

Kapi regained his composure and began, 'Coming back to honouring Muktak ...'

Sheru was full of enthusiasm. 'What a great honour sir! You will get to carry Mr Leader on your back!'

'*Will you keep quiet?*' screamed Muktak.

Kapi thought that the scream was meant for him, so he enquired.

'Sorry, it was not for you. Anyway, what if I refuse to be honoured, Mr Leader?'

Sheru whispered with urgency, 'Do not refuse it, sir. I will feel privileged to have right connections in high places.'

With great difficulty Muktak restrained himself from kicking Sheru.

Kapi knew about honours and laurels, but he did not know about the rules of refusal. He first looked foolishly here and there, and then responded, 'We will tear you to pieces.'

'But that goes against the second principle of junglezens, "good of all, growth of all". By tearing me to pieces, you won't be doing any good to me,' laughed Muktak.

This further confused Kapi. He finally said, 'You refuse honour from us and we refuse to accept your existence. We will ignore you. We will definitely ignore you. There is no way that we will not ignore you.'

'Suits me.'

'What are you doing, sir? I will be known as the disciple of "nobody". Please do not do so in my interest.' Sheru desperately tried to reason with Muktak but all in vain.

Dholu began instructing his pupils with a glowing tribute to the motherland, the idea of junglezen, and the Leader.

Sheru was happy to be in the new system of mass education. This offered him novelty and the company of zens of his age. The young ones were from every breed, and they brought with them a potful of ideas, strengths, weaknesses, ambitions and fears. The idea of junglezen demanded that all these be boiled together to bring out a grand concoction which would not have the distinctive smell of any particular group. The job required tenacity that only a donkey could display.

'Young zens! Say "A",' Dholu would shout in the class.

'A,' the young ones would repeat with innocent devotion in their own distinctive voices and tones.

'That won't do. Full throated, full throated. No bleating or squeaking.'

There was a deer fawn in the class, Hiru. He protested at the persistence of his teacher, 'Sir, I can only bleat. My throat is too delicate to bray. What should I do?'

'Bray, bray, and bray. If you fail, then bray again. That is the way to success.'

Sheru was fascinated by Hiru, who appeared to him as the ultimate in beauty, straightforwardness, and courage. He offered to be friends with the fawn, but Hiru was not so sure, 'My mom says that friendship and enmity should be between equals. And you do not seem my equal. You do not even have beautiful spots like I have all over my body.'

Sheru whimpered, 'I had those spots when I was very young. They are gone now. Please do not reject me simply because I do not have spots.'

'And you eat meat.'

'I will give that up right away. I promise to live on roots and fruits forever. Will you reconsider now?' He was ready to do anything to fit in to what Hiru desired. 'I will check with my mom. She does not like me to hobnob with zens who have no family background.'

'I come from the lion family.'

'Maybe. But we have not seen your parents, and I personally do not believe in tales such as lion. Anyway, you can always be my classmate.'

Sheru had to remain content by admiring Hiru from a distance. In his zeal to be accepted by the deer, he was prepared to get spots all over his body by any means. He even thought of asking Kaak to do him this favour, but the fear of Muktak stopped him from doing that.

Every evening, Sheru updated Muktak about his progress at school, which was not at all encouraging. Instead of focussing on his core strength, Sheru was spending his time making friends with fawns, rodents, squirrels, monkeys, and donkeys.

'It is alright to associate with your unequal. But socializing with your inferiors is a silly thing to do. In social interaction, hearts of both sides open for give and take. You are a lion. Someday, you will have to be the king of the forest. So stop this silly business of socializing with your inferiors.'

'Junglezen Muktak sir! We are all junglezens. There is no lion.'

'Don't call me junglezen again if you value your life. You yourself are lying in the mud, and you want to drag others to your level too.'

'Suits me. But we are all junglezens, and we are all equal.'

'There is nothing called junglezen, nor is there anything called equality. Everyone has an essence – just like the essence of fire is its heat. Strength is your essence. That is your core. That is you. Focus only on that. If you lose your essence, you will become a waste; if you compromise with your strength, you will be left only with weakness.'

Sheru kept mum. 'I do not want to hear stories about you socializing with rats and cats in future. My mom used to say that every personality is like milk and everyone around him is like water. If you can bring out your core, you become like butter. You can then mix freely with anyone. But if you mix with those around you without gaining your essence, you will then end up becoming like diluted milk.'

'Yes, sir.' Sheru replied politely. *Why argue with those who do not appreciate the changing winds of time?* he thought silently.

To please his masters, the one at the school

and at home, Sheru developed unique ways to adopt different personalities in different places. That way everyone was happy.

A meet was organized for the guardians to watch the progress of their young ones at Dholu's academy.

Junglezens from all over the forest came to watch the event, and encourage their kids to win prizes. The meet was to be graced by the entire council headed by Kapi. To show respect to each one of the council members, the school authorities came up with titles like chief guest, guest-in-chief, honoured, special, venerable, etc. guest. It all sounded silly but that ensured that there were no frayed nerves among the powerful.

The programme began with 'Jai Junglezen!' – a song in praise of the paradigmatic shift in the forest. Everyone liked it, but many were surprised to hear the young zens trying to bray in imitation of their teacher. Many others thought that probably the song was set on some kind of modern experimental music. They appreciated the effort.

Hiru's mother was sitting near Muktak. She felt uneasy about the style of singing and expressed it to him. Muktak smiled, 'When apes are leaders, aping becomes the cult.' The lady maintained an annoyed silence. She did not find anything funny about her child learning to bray instead of bleat.

Rig was then invited to say a few words of inspiration to the learners. He began, 'Young zens! Our sacred land has been the mother of all that there is in the world. Even human civilization has flowed out from here. We have exported material, mind, and wisdom from here. Unfortunately, our land has been exploited for a long time by the unscrupulous.'

Rig stopped for a moment to look at Muktak and Sheru, and then continued, 'The lion killed in the name of protection, and the elephants looted in the name of doing service. All that has changed now and only the relics of these families remain. We have achieved the impossible by sacrificing everything for you. We now expect you to carry the torch of liberty and unity. Jai Junglezen!'

The crowed echoed, 'Jai Junglezen!'

Rig sat down with a straight back, Sheru hung his head in shame, and Muktak stood erect with dignity.

With formalities over, it was time for the audience to watch the achievements of the young ones.

Sheru, along with his mates, stood on the starting line for the race. At the sound of the whistle, they all sprinted to win the prize from the minister. The shouts, screams, and yells by the spectators filled them with unbound energy.

Hiru ran fast. Very fast.

Sheru had been upset at the mention of his family as killers. But being young, his negative emotions were cleared by the new activities that followed the next moment. He was happy at the prospect of running alongside Hiru, so he ran fast and caught up with him.

'Hi Hiru!'

'This is not the time to talk,' Hiru panted.

Muktak looked at Sheru with bemused eyes. He could never make Sheru run, but here he was running like lightning with his friend.

Sheru and Hiru were leading the race. It was difficult to say which one of the two would win. All other kids were left far behind.

The gathering was clapping to cheer them on when there was a sharp whistle by Dholu – the signal to stop the race. Dholu asked the participants to return to the starting line.

When all had reached back, Dholu began, pain dripping from his voice, 'It is a disgrace! How many times have I talked to you about equality and dignity! How well have I trained you in these arts? And, here you are! Outrunning each other! Shame! You have let me down!'

The cub and the fawn hung their head in shame.

When the race began afresh, every participant trotted to keep pace with the slowest moving member.

Hiru's mom refused to take it anymore. She screamed, 'Stop this nautanki. I do not want my precious to learn the stupid things of mass education. I am withdrawing my child. Now.'

Kapi and Dholu tried to reason with her. But who in the world could calm an angry mom? 'When danger comes, will this equality and dignity save my precious child? Off with your ideas. I will have my son tutored privately.'

Muktak agreed with Hiru's mom, 'I think individuality should be encouraged.'

The loud dissent of Muktak boomed through the crowd. This infuriated Kapi. 'You are hogwash, long nose. Keep your mouth shut. You had your days. Now the public rules.'

Kapi's comments hurt the boar who now came forward to object. 'Mr Leader sir! You have no right to use the word "hogwash". I find the term insulting.'

'I did not mean to insult you. I hope you understand.'

'No, I do not understand that, nor do I care to understand. Apologize for your "hogwash" comment.'

'Now look. I never said anything like that.'

'What? You did not say that?'

'I did not mean to say that I did not say that. I meant to say something, but the meaning to you was different.'

'Did you, or did you not say "hogwash"?'

More words created more confusion which created more words. Finally the celebration ended in a grand confusion.

To get a clear perspective on the issue, Sheru asked Muktak on their way back, 'Sir, are you, or are you not hogwash?'

An angry Muktak raised his trunk, 'Learn silence if you cannot talk sense. Or do you want a hammering?'

Hiru left Dholu's school. Within a few days, more pupils left the school for private education. Soon only donkeys were left to give company to Sheru.

After Hiru's departure from the school, Sheru

started growing more and more listless. He missed his friend badly.

When Muktak could not bear it anymore, he decided to give him a pep talk. 'Years ago when I was young ...'

Sheru interrupted, 'Now that is what is called a tall talk. Do not try to convince me that you were also young.'

Muktak's seniority made many think that he had always been like that. Yes, he was the oldest among them all, and was even older than the grandfather and great grandfather of most of them. Due to this, many thought that he was eternal and had actually planted the forest. But that was not true. There were many trees in the forest which were a witness to his childhood pranks. Once upon a time he loved to roll in the dust, which invariably got him a good spanking from his mother.

Muktak smiled at Sheru. 'You may not care to know, but only young ones are born in our forest. Is that okay?' Muktak said smilingly, and then continued, 'I was once going through an identity crisis. One day, I met an elderly camel who had escaped the city and had come to the forest. Initially, no one noticed his speciality, but slowly it dawned upon everyone that he had a special calm about him. So I approached him for a discussion.

Mr Camel said, "I have seen the world." This was his standard statement.

"I agree sir. Your sagging skin indicates that. But how do you stay so calm?"

"As I said – I have seen the world. I have worked in the war fields where canons boomed, and life could be lost for a pittance. I have traversed through deserts for days together without taking a drop of water. I acquired and lost; I also lost and acquired."

"Sir, I was not asking about your life story."

"After all the journeys of life, I learnt that the best thing in life is to stay free, and also to allow freedom to those around myself. Now I stand calm and content," concluded Mr Camel.

From that day I have practised the motto of "stay free, allow freedom" to maintain my calm. I realized that only kids hold on to their toys and cry when it is taken away.'

'Freedom! Freedom! It is all rotten papaya.'

'Sheru, learn to let go. What is rightfully yours will come back to you. There is no force in the universe that can stop you from getting what is yours.'

Sheru whimpered, 'So, how is it that Hiru is not with me?'

'You cannot keep something confined to you if

it does not belong to you. Grow up, Sheru. Learn freedom, learn to let go.'

'Your words are good only for the decrepit. I have no use for them.

'Suffer then. It is a package deal, young zen. Chase the chimera and shed tears.'

'I will prefer that, Master. It is better to shed tears for what one does not get than to want nothing in life to stay calm. Your fossilized wisdom is not for us moderns.'

'Meaningless to reason with the volatile,' Muktak sighed and changed the topic.

III

Teachers 'n' Teachers

'A good student learns after hearing once from the master, a mediocre student needs repeated instructions, and a bad student misinterprets the teaching.'

– Acharya Shankara

With Hiru gone from the school, Sheru had no incentive left to continue at Dholu's school. For some days, he continued going there irregularly, and then stopped going altogether. Every morning, he now bid goodbye to Muktak for the school but instead of going there, he loitered around the forest exploring inconsequential things.

'Nothing like exploration. It gives you character. It makes you an educated zen,' Sheru convinced himself. Muktak knew nothing about these developments.

One day, Sheru was hiding behind a tree, listening for Muktak's steps to avoid him, when Shuka, the parrot, fell on him from the branch where he had been sitting and dozing.

Unlike other parrots who merely repeated words, Shuka claimed to be a philosopher. He talked a lot, and like a true babbler, he fell asleep whenever he was not talking. His sleep was always fitful because of his excessive chatter, so he dreamt a lot, and whatever came to him in those dreamy states, he claimed them to be enlightening truths. Birds were not interested in his junk, but they tolerated him because they felt that a philosopher amidst them brought prestige to their tribe.

That day, Shuka had been sitting on a tree and musing on the nothingness of life. As he contemplated, his mind travelled and he began to think about emptiness, and then about the cosmic void. This lulled him into a deep dreamy state in which he came up with the conclusion that there is nothing called creation. This realization and his dreamy state made him lose his grip on the branch. On his way down, he could have used his wings like any other bird to escape a fall, but his semi-enlightened mode did not allow him to be sure if his fall was for real, or whether he was merely experiencing nothingness.

The shock of fall brought Shuka from the unreal to the real. Embarrassed, he told Sheru, 'There is a special meaning to my fall.'

Sheru, who was bunking school by tricking his guardian and his teacher, was not dumb. He knew that there was nothing special about the parrot's fall but he still commented, 'Yes, sir. Probably, sir. Maybe definitely, sir.'

'You will be a great learner, young zen.'

'Thank you, sir.'

'I knew your father well.'

'My father. Ah!' The topic always made him emotional.

'He was a perfect gentleman. What power! What strength!'

'I wish I had those qualities.'

'I can teach you in a day all that is to be learnt about strength, power, fight, victory, etc. I am the only expert in these areas. All this was revealed to me by the higher forces of nature.'

It does not take long for the self-impressed to impress the gullible. Sheru was no exception. He was ready to be impressed. 'That would be great, sir. Please. Mr Muktak makes me work hard to learn things. He says that there is no short cut to success, and that easy come easy go.'

'Hard work, my fallen feather!' Shuka thundered. 'Brute force has never ruled the world. Intellect, Sheru, intellect. Intellect has ruled the world, and will rule it forever. Knowledge is power, wealth, glory – everything. Have faith in me, and you will be the master of your destiny and the destiny of others by the power of your intellect.'

Like most hollow philosophers, Shuka had

mastered the art of speaking since his early days. Since most birds are talkers themselves, Shuka never got a proper audience. Now with a committed listener in Sheru, he got down vigorously to stretching ideas, squeezing points, giving extra pauses, and puffing off.

Shuka considered the number eleven to be divine. This had been 'revealed' to him in one of his dreamy states. So, whenever he had to use numbers, he used eleven, and occasionally its multiples. He believed that there were eleven worlds, eleven gods, eleven oceans, etc., and according to him, the world was to come to an end after eleven hundred springs. He recommended his folks to have eleven wives, and eleven kids from each one of them. This had annoyed the females of his species and he had to live the life of a helpless bachelor.

After Shuka had finished, Sheru thanked him wholeheartedly, 'I cannot tell you, sir, how enlightened I feel after your talk. There is a new burst of energy within me, and I feel like conquering the world. I wonder how our folks missed learning from you. It is indeed true that a bird will never be respected by other birds.'

'You are already talking sense. Go, conquer the world.'

In the evening when Sheru met Muktak,

positivity was oozing out from his every limb. 'Do you know, Master, there are eleven ways of attack, and eleven ways of defence in any fight?'

Muktak took time to grasp the situation. He could not believe that Sheru had been bunking school for so many days. His ocean of surprise produced only a single wave of 'I see'.

'Yes. I can attack you at eleven spots in eleven different ways. To ward off your attack, I can take eleven steps in defence,' said Sheru excitedly.

Muktak was getting back his wit. With sheer disgust, he said, 'Wonderful. Now come and attack me. Let me see the art of your warfare. I promise not to stir from my spot.'

Sheru advanced towards Muktak, initially with confidence, and then hesitatingly. For every step forward, he now took two steps backwards.

'Come, you coward! Attack, or I will kill you!' Muktak trumpeted. He was not sure why he was feeling frustrated. Probably at his own failure as a mentor.

The fear of an angry Muktak filled Sheru with a sudden burst of nervous energy. He charged. Muktak moved his trunk effortlessly, curled it around Sheru's body, and lifted him off the ground.

'Should I now throw you eleven miles away?'

'You must not do that. I am your only disciple. You will never get another one like me.'

'How many escape routes from such a situation might there be, Master Sheru?'

'I think eleven, sir. But release me. Please.'

'That I will. I have no intentions of keeping a snail hanging from my trunk. But remember that there has never been a shortcut to success, you stupid.'

Muktak then put Sheru down, who ran to a safe distance. From there he said confidently, 'See how I tricked you into letting me go. This is one of the eleven ways of escape. And with due respect sir, I was caught off guard because it was a mock fight. I will surely be much more careful in actual fights. There is nothing wrong with my knowledge and learning.'

Sheru refused to go to school anymore. This was fine with Muktak, but Sheru also found ways to escape his training.

One day, he was sitting under a tree, thinking about this and that when he was greeted with 'Jai Junglezen!' It was Gillu, the squirrel, the great admirer of Muktak.

Sheru responded half-heartedly. He did not

care much for those who could not teach him something great, something special.

'What a pleasure meeting you. I knew your father well. What manliness!' Gillu said.

'My father. Ah!' said Sheru wistfully.

'Yes. I have also been a longtime friend and admirer of your mentor, Muktak.'

'Please do not talk about him. He makes me work hard, and lectures me in his free time. He says that I must attain strength to face challenges. What does he mean by that? Don't I have strength? Can't I crush you with my paw?'

Gillu had no desire to be crushed under Sheru's paw. He climbed up to a higher branch and said, 'Oh, that is nothing. I know all about defence.'

That interested Sheru. 'Could you please teach me the art of defence, sir? I will remain ever obliged to you.'

'Ha! Ha! It is so simple.'

'Really? How?'

'Whenever in danger, just "touch wood".'

'I did not get you.'

'Whenever we are in danger, we just run for the nearest tree. This is called "touching wood". The monkeys also do the same, and I have heard from Kaak that most city folks touch wood whenever they are temporarily afraid, or whenever they wish to be permanently protected. Of course they also say "touch wood" aloud, which we do not. Probably that is what gives them an edge over us.'

'What an enlightening truth! I wonder why you have not broadcast it.'

'Some knowledge should be kept esoteric. Just see how city folks have become so powerful by learning our secret.'

'That is great, sir. I will get down to mastering the art of "touching wood" right away.'

Sheru, the selective-serious sort that he was, got down to practising what he had just learnt.

In the evening, when Sheru did not return home, Muktak came out in search of him, and found him under a tree, jumping up and down shouting 'touch wood' and trying unsuccessfully to climb the tree. He was bruised and covered all over with dirt.

When Muktak came to know about this, he screamed in anger, 'The next time I see you believing any mumbo jumbo, I will throw you upon a high tree where you can "touch wood" till you die of hunger and thirst.'

The lessons with Shuka and Gillu had not gone off well for Sheru. But that did not deter him from his search for a teacher who could get him success and glory easily.

One day, Sheru was standing under a tree when he felt a weight crushing him around his body, and lifting him up in mid-air. He shrieked.

He found himself caught in the coils of the forest python. This giant of a snake, measuring more than ten metres, stayed around that tree, and when he was hungry, no one who passed his way was safe.

The python considered himself special for reasons not accepted by others. He boasted that he was the only being whose growth was indeterminate – he would continue to grow till he died. Every other animal suffered from degenerative process, but he did not. He attributed this speciality to his belly power, about which he was truly proud.

'Belly! Belly is everything. Focus on your belly, and you will be the king.'

His frequency of hunger depended on the size of his last meal. Once he had his fill, he lay inert for days to enjoy his acquisition. About this habit of his, he would say, 'Only the depraved eat every day. The truly great do not indulge in such wasteful exercise.'

After the mandatory period of rest following his meal, he was generally full of cheer, and talked a lot about his greatness to anyone who would hear him. 'I am great because I do not discriminate. I grab the sitting, creeping, running, swimming, and flying. I am truly democratic, you see.'

'Do not conclude that those whom I eat suffer a great loss,' he would say. 'They become one with me – the greatest one around. I am the king of the species which has been specially created by the Lord. We are superior to the "leggies" who hobble around. And why legs only? Sense organs themselves are aberrations. The more organs you have, the more incompetent you become. None of the five great elements – ether, air, fire, water, earth – has legs, or any other sense organ. Nor do the sun, moon, stars, and planets have those. That is what makes me great. I am the greatest. I am the best. Whomsoever I put in my belly becomes one with my greatness. Lucky them!'

Those who did not believe his words were devoured by him. 'You can verify this when in my belly,' he would say.

Sheru was gasping when he felt the gaping mouth approach him. The python looked closely at him, and then slackened his grip.

'Sir, release me, sir. I will never come this way again.' Sheru pleaded and prayed.

To the astonishment of Sheru, Mr Python said,

'Worry not. I will not kill you. You are the only child of my good old friend Mr Lion, the former king of the forest. You may not know, but I am the king of the reptile world. We kings have a code that we never attack the families of each other. When in danger, we even look after their kin. So, you are safe with me. I caught you by mistake.'

The python then loosened the grip further.

Sheru's father may have been friends with this creature from the underworld, but being a confirmed idealist, Sheru was intolerant of the views of others. He politely said, 'Sir, there are no lions, no kings. There are only junglezens now. '

'See! See! How I learn by squeezing the dying! Junglezen! Ha! I have heard the term, but do not understand anything about it. Help me by explaining.' Mr Python claimed that he had immense practical knowledge, which came to him through what he ate. 'Before I eat someone, I learn everything from him by squeezing him tightly. What others think as cries, are, in fact, the words of wisdom passed on to me by my partners in synergetic entrepreneurship,' he would say.

Sheru explained, 'In this forest, we are all equals, and we are known as junglezens. Collectivism is our ideal now. We do not differentiate one from the other.'

Mr Python laughed out so loudly that Sheru fell out of his grip.

He then said, 'The demand for equality has been the eternal cry of the weaklings. But whenever destiny made the mistake of granting equality to the weak with the strong, that society was soon overrun by the barbarians. That is how the good of that particular society perished with the scum – in sameness.'

Sheru felt angry at being contradicted. Mr Python continued.

'In our snake world, once the green snakes, worthless that they are, started a movement for equality. What did I do then? I, the king of the reptile world … Well, I agreed fully with them, and ate up the whole lot to give them permanent equality in my stomach. Since then, I have not heard murmurs of equality in my world.'

Sheru had no intentions of attaining that kind of equality. Thinking that Mr Python was lost in his garrulity like an old person, he moved slowly towards his escape.

Sheru had misjudged the situation. The reptile was not only alert, but also agile. He caught Sheru again and said, 'If I want to finish you, I can track you down anywhere in the forest and be done with you. So, no need to run away. I am indeed your well-wisher, and will be happy to be your teacher in more than one way.'

'Thank you, sir.'

'Come out of your strange ideas of equality. If you compromise with your strength, you will be left only with weakness.'

'Excuse me, sir. Did you go to the same school as my mentor, Muktak? He also tells me the same thing.'

Mr Python laughed. 'No. I did not go to school. No achiever ever goes to school. And thank you for telling me about Muktak. How is he? I am a great admirer of his wisdom. It's a pity that he did not become the king of the forest.'

'We do not have kings anymore.'

Mr Python felt annoyed at the obstinacy of Sheru, and so allowed him to leave, with an open invitation to visit him anytime.

When Sheru informed Muktak about the incident, he said, 'Yes, it is true that he won't harm you. But his views are too gross for my sensibilities. He is clever. And like every clever fellow, he is not wise. He values only himself – the crass materialist.'

So it was ironic that soon Mr Python became

Sheru's grand teacher. Like his long belly that unfolded slowly, his knowledge too started unfolding before the learner.

The forest, rich with its produce of roots, fruits and shoots, kept its folks well fed, gently behaved, and amply bred. Easy food gave zens plenty of free time, and good rest filled them with energy. The worthy used their time to philosophize while the unworthy probed the affairs of others. Barak, the goat was a serious type. A philosopher.

Barak also thought highly of his species because even the females had beards. But the lion, when he was alive, had never paid any attention to this unique trait of his family. That had always hurt Barak. When the process of electing a new leader was going on, he had objected to the idea for the fear of being ignored again. 'Better to have no leader than to have a leader who ignores you.'

Whenever free, Barak would stand under some tree and muse on the uncertainties of life. Kaak, the regular visitor to the city, had told the forest that there were many in the city who behaved like Barak and were known as philosophers and saints, but were actually world beaten. They could be found sitting on the banks of the river, praying inside the temples, or lying under the shade of trees. These otherworldly humans had lost all faith in themselves, and now either depended on God, or waited for death.

When Barak heard about those folks of the city, he was filled with enthusiasm, and wanted to be like them. This led him to come up with his signature statement, 'It is bad enough to be born, but it is worse to live long.' Unfortunately for him, his profound thought had few takers.

The search for a perfect teacher brought Sheru to Barak.

'I knew your father well. It is unfortunate that he did not value my speciality.'

'My father. Ah!'

'Thinkers should be honoured by the royal court. That is the only way a kingdom can survive. If Mr Lion had valued my opinions, he would have been alive and hunting today.'

'Sir, your words are inspiring. I wish to be your disciple.'

'Life is a misery.'

'I know that from my personal experience, sir. What a great thinker you must be! You must have suffered a lot to attain such wisdom.'

'Yes, young zen. My life has been a series of

sufferings. Starting from my birth, to marriage, I have been suffering and suffering. The powerful ignore me, the weak ridicule me, my own avoid me, and death eludes me.'

'What is the way out, sir?' asked a visibly impressed Sheru.

'Many. There are many ways to escape these burdens of life. I will teach you all that I have acquired. But right now, I have to collect a secret message from Magar for Rig. I am not supposed to talk about it to anyone, but since you are my disciple, you are my own. You can come to the river and stay at a distance till I finish my job.'

'Gladly, sir, I have only heard of Mr Magar, but have never seen him. It is my lucky day.'

They both walked towards the river. When they reached the bank, Sheru stood at a distance to avoid listening to State secrets.

The greedy are rarely lazy. So when Barak called out for the crocodile, he appeared instantly.

'Ah, finally your turn today! I have been waiting to see you from the days of the first forest gathering when that fatso elephant drove me away from you.'

Barak philosophized a lot. This demanded silence. Through the practice of maintaining silence over long periods he had developed a strong sixth sense. His intuition told him that there was danger around. He became cautious and did not stir from his place.

'Come nearer,' commanded Magar. 'I can convey the confidential message only in your ears.'

The suspicion was turning into a conviction. 'There is no one around, sir. You can say it out loud.'

The greedy are also impatient. In sheer frustration, Magar made a dash for Barak. 'Sheru!' screamed a terrified Barak.

Sheru was alert. He immediately responded to the alarm of his teacher. 'Sir!' His voice boomed across the river.

The sudden roar of a lion terrified Magar. He had been an old fighter, and the forest lore was that he had once dragged a bison into the river. But when it came to a lion, Magar always lost his nerves. There was something in a lion's appearance and his roar that made a coward of the bravest. Magar now lost his nerve and dived for the deep.

When Sheru narrated the river episode to Muktak, he commented, 'Secret message indeed! This monkey will ruin our land. It is his ploy to send the unsuspecting to the vile.'

Rig found it surprising that Barak was alive. He was even more surprised when he saw that whomever he sent to Magar in the next few days, only returned to inform that there had neither been any message, nor any trace of Magar in the river.

Barak did not say much to anyone, but he knew that he had escaped certain death. Surprisingly, this changed his perception towards life and death. He suddenly started to find that life was full of cheer.

The rumour of there being an unholy nexus between the powerful and the demanding spread thick over the forest. Soon it became so thick that junglezens found it difficult to breathe anything other than that rumour. There were only uncharitable comments and opinions in the forest against the monkey-jackal administration. This slowly turned into public anger, which ultimately led to a massive protest against them.

'Down with the killer lot!' shouted the head.

'Blood for blood!' the body responded.

Kapi was terrified. He had faced booing and hissing in circus, but this situation was terrifying. 'Performers can be achievers only with the captive crowd,' he concluded, and thought of abdicating. But that option was too painful for him. 'Power, sweet power, what will I be sans you! Nothing. Better to die than to give up.'

Rig came running when he heard of the protests, and consoled Kapi. 'Do not worry, friend! Relax. Enjoy. I will handle this with the ABCD of administration.'

That Rig had addressed him as 'friend' was an insult according to Kapi. How could he be a 'friend' of his subordinate? But the thought that Rig might have a solution made Kapi ignore the offence.

'What is ABCD?'

'Avoid. Bypass. Committee. Delay.' Rig then whispered a few things to Kapi which brightened him up.

Kapi went to face the crowd, 'Friends! Junglezen! Brothers! What is all this noise about? Do you want us to go on a wild goose chase instead of working for your welfare? We are here only for you, but is it proper for you to waste our precious time on issues that do not even exist? There has never been any killing by Mr Magar nor will there ever be. He is our only ally in the outside world, so these are nothing but nasty allegations.

'Down with empty words. Hang the culprits!' shouted the crowd.

'Well, we all know which non-progressive forces are working against us. I will not name them since you know them well. But I wish to remind these dark forces that there is a thing called destiny. These forces will be annihilated under the sway of the unforgiving.'

Kapi turned his head around to see the impact of his own words. Yes, some were charmed.

'Blood for blood!' shouted the crowd.

It had not worked perfectly, so Kapi had to move on to plan B. Bypass. He began, 'There might have been an accident or two. Why this fuss over that? We have so much to do, so much to achieve, and here you are wasting your collective energy. C'mon! Get up. Let us build a new futuristic society. Up, up with you!'

'We want justice!' shouted the crowd. Many had lost their dear ones.

On to C.

'Fine. If you insist on wasting our resources, it is alright. We will form a committee here and now to investigate the matter. You suggest names of some elderly and wise junglezens. There will be no interference from the administration. We will be there only to guide the members to make the findings foolproof. Action will be taken on the basis of the findings of the committee. Responsible that you all are, you must realize that we cannot punish the innocent simply because of the insistence of those with vested interests.'

The crowd had to agree to this proposal.

'Now for D,' Rig let out a twisted smile. 'The elderly never like to give up their position, so we will keep extending their term of enquiry. In case the report is ready, we will have enough dissent notes on it. And, if that too fails, then we can always delay the implementation. Nothing like D!'

Kapi relaxed.

The committee was formed and it immediately got down to serious work. The forest lore is that it is still working on it and organizing the facts to file a comprehensive report.

The forest folks, of course, realized that they had to fend for themselves. They stopped paying attention to Rig's request of going to the river to get the secret information.

Rig did not forget that Sheru was directly linked with the crocodile affair. 'That rascal has to be removed from the path of the royal affairs,' Rig hissed, and then he came up with a grand plan which could not fail.

For all practical purposes, Sheru was now out of Rig's way.

IV

The Royal Mount

*Your future is determined by what your actions
and what your understanding have been ...*
                                                    – Kathopanishad

A bad teacher makes you work hard, but a good teacher leads you to success without labour – this was Sheru's understanding of education. He was not alone in thinking so; most kids thought the same, but their parents disciplined them into seeing otherwise.

The failure to get such a perfect teacher made Sheru roam the forest more and more. That is how he met Rig one day, who was also out in search of him.

'Looking for a teacher, Junglezen Sheru?'

'Yes, sir.'

'I knew your father well, and had accompanied him in many of his hunting expeditions. He was quite satisfied with my skills.'

Rig did not say that he had always followed the lion only with the safety of distance between them. He also did not care to mention that he had to share the lion's leftovers with Kaak, which had been the cause of many quarrels between them.

'My father. Ah!'

'A great leader he was. Yes, he was a great leader. Today, I am able to run the affairs of our land only because I practise what little I had picked up from your father.'

'I am touched by your kind words, sir.'

'You can also be a great leader if you follow the principles of leadership.'

'Sir?'

'After serving Mr Lion, serving our present leader is ... well ...'

'Sir?'

'Let me explain to you the important things of life and leadership through a comparison between the good and the bad.'

'That will be great, sir. I can then face Mr Muktak with my head held high.'

'Don't take that senile tusker's name in front of me. He has ruined our land by eating all that is good here and he has doomed you by destroying all that is good in you.'

Nothing excites a young mind more than receiving encouragement for his views, even if those are stupid. Sheru glowed, 'Yes, sir. He wants me to work hard for my success. But that is sure to destroy all that is good in me. Tell me, sir, how can I ever attain success if all that is good in me is destroyed?'

Rig wondered how Muktak tolerated this cucumber-head. However, when the goal is set, one has to tread the path, easy or difficult, with tenacity. Rig continued, 'Back to our discussion.

Mr Lion never had a coterie to run his empire. The whisper is that he did consult your mom, but that is something pardonable.'

'My mom!'

'And see our leader! He is always surrounded by sycophants. These sycophants will bring his ruin someday. Mark my words.'

'What is a sycophant, sir?' Sheru had no idea about such exalted concepts.

Rig was a confirmed tyrant to his subordinates. And like every tyrant, he was a perfect sycophant to his masters. He knew this well and also knew that others knew that. This made him wonder if Sheru also knew, and was only acting as if he did not.

Playing safe, he scolded Sheru for distracting him and continued, 'We do all the hard work, but Mr Leader wants all the credit for himself. He never gives what is due to us. I have heard somewhere that "Give him what is his", but our great leader believes in "Take from him what is his". What a shame that we have to work for such a despot!'

'Sir …'

Seeing that Sheru was being unresponsive, Rig changed track.

'Let me tell you an incident from your father's times. Once I was following Mr Lion on an expedition. It so happened that he was angry for some reason and let out a fierce roar. Would you believe that his roar could be heard more than ten miles away? I heard it myself, and the same was later confirmed by many others. Also, the force of his roar had flattened the grass near him, and had made the leaves of the nearby trees tremble!'

Sheru felt good.

'And yet,' Rig continued, 'he would never roar at us. He knew that a leader who raises his voice is not a true leader. His mere presence and a glance was enough to tame the most errant.'

'Ah!'

'And look at our present leader. This monkey of a leader keeps gritting his teeth, makes faces, raises his voice, uses expletives, and keeps saying, "You do not know me, you do not know me!" Tell me, what is there to know of him – the monkey?'

Sheru interrupted, 'Sir, I believe that one must not hear things about the leader. The boss can do no wrong; he is never wrong.'

Kaak had been flying around in search of juicy bits of news when he noticed the cub-fox duo engaged in a chat. Giving a break to his professionalism, he cawed, 'Be careful Sheru. Rig is an old hand at cunning. Don't listen to him. No good will come of it.'

Rig was already feeling frustrated with Sheru for delaying his mission. Now his old rivalry with Kaak, and the present insults made him howl furiously, 'Even coal can be made white by burning, but nothing can cleanse your dark deeds, you darky!'

'Manipulation and anger do not go together, you foxy. You better stick to what is your speciality – cunning. And listen, Sheru! I was the one to find you, so I feel responsible towards you. Beware of this sly fur coat. He can only bring disaster to you.'

Kaak crowed for a while, cursing Rig and encouraging Sheru. When he found that nothing was coming out of it, he let out a big curse and flew away.

An agitated Rig continued, 'Many obstacles come in the path of greatness, Sheru. Wonder not at the failures, rather learn to marvel at success.'

'A great statement, sir! You are a true teacher!'

'Yes. So, do you now realize how our leader is not acting properly?'

'I know nothing about him, sir.'

'You doubt my words, you dolt? Junglezen Sheru, it is your sacred duty to serve your land with utmost sincerity. Grow up for once. Be bold. Be honest. Admit that a leader should be fair.'

'Yes sir. A leader should be fair.'

'An unfair leader should not be allowed to hold position. After all, it is not his life that matters, but the life of millions. What do you say?'

'Definitely, sir.'

Rig let out the smile of the satisfied. He had achieved his goal. Sheru was now as good as finished. He said, 'That is it. You will go far in life.'

'I am honoured, sir.'

Rig then embraced Sheru, with a show of great emotion. 'I am your true well-wisher, young zen. Come to me for anything you need. I cannot replace your father, but I will always be there for you. Do remember me when you become someone great, which you will, one day. And, keep our talk a secret. I trust you.'

After meeting Sheru, Rig went straight to Kapi and lamented in an anguished tone, 'Mr Leader sir! We are done for! We are heading for trouble. Sheru is becoming anti-establishment. He just now told me that your leadership is not fair, and that you should be dethroned.'

He then detailed his report with truth, semi-truth and untruths. He talked loudly, softly, in a raised voice, and in whispers to emphasize various aspects of the conspiracy. By the time he had finished, Kapi was trembling with shock, fright, and anger.

Sheru was asked to report to the royal court. This made him nervous. 'No good ever happens when the king meets the commoner,' he thought worriedly.

In the court, he faced the council. Dholu, his old teacher, was present as a member. Bhalu, Rig, and many others were also present.

Kapi began in a flat tone, 'I knew your relatives when I was into performing arts. They were so obedient and disciplined.' He could suppress his violent emotions only with great difficulty.

'Thank you, Mr Leader. I will always cherish your words as the highest compliment for my family and me.'

'So, how is it that we are hearing complaints about your indiscipline?'

Sheru thought that the complaint had something to do with his leaving Dholu's school. 'Sorry sir. I am truly sorry about that. I will do as you order, but why should such trifles come to your high office?'

'You call it trifle?' Kapi screamed in anger. All his fear was flowing out in the form of volcanic anger, and position had added authority to his voice. 'And you are also trying to learn the art of leadership!'

A confused Sheru tried to understand the words. His mind was still stuck on the idea of the donkey's school. He looked quizzically at Dholu, and then at Kapi, but could not understand what it was all about.

Kapi thundered, 'Do you know what leadership is all about? Indigestion, insomnia, and insults. And you want these for yourself? You fool! Let these remain with me. Let me suffer so that you can thrive.' His voice was choking.

Sheru had no desire to suffer indigestion and insomnia. Insults were a different matter. He was learning well to live with them. 'But what has that to do with the school?' he wondered.

Kapi continued, 'A true junglezen is one who loves and serves his people. But you should know that people are governed by the system, and the system is run by the leader. So, if you serve the leader, you automatically serve your people. Serving the leader is the right way to show your gratitude to your land and your people. You are failing in that.'

A confused Sheru could not make anything of this discourse on political philosophy. But the scalding words of Kapi made him feel weak in legs. He asked nervously, 'May I sit down sir? My head is reeling.' He did not wait for the permission, and collapsed on a seat.

Kapi ignored the plight of Sheru, and continued, 'From today, you will be directly under my supervision. You will carry me wherever I go, and you will guard my place when I am here. Learn to serve the leader, and someday you yourself will become a leader.'

Kapi had not abandoned his desire to be carried by someone important. 'What is a leader if he cannot be recognized by his convoy and outriders?' He now felt happy that destiny had given him the opportunity to sate his vanity.

Sheru was terribly confused now. Initially, he had been under the impression that he was being punished for something, but here he was being given such a great honour! Carrying Mr Leader! So what was all that hullabaloo about? It is truly said that weird are the ways of a leader.'

Aloud he said, 'Thank you sir. I feel honoured.' A new wave of energy started coursing through him.

Once released from the court, he ran to Muktak with the great news. Powered by excitement and expectation, he raced through the forest like never before. The wind whizzing past his body got heated. His yellow figure, sloth under normal conditions, appeared like a yellow arrow shot by an Olympian. Every animal, big or small, scurried away in fright. The older ones had nearly forgotten how it felt when a lion ran and the new generation had never seen a lion run.

Oblivious of his own power, and its effect on others, Sheru reached Muktak and exclaimed, 'Good news from your good-for-nothing disciple, sir!'

'Yes, I can see that you have finally learnt to run the way you should.'

'Oh, that is nothing. I could do that anytime. The real news is much more exciting.'

He then narrated all that had happened a while ago, and said proudly, 'Your disciple is now the royal guard, and the royal mount. I have achieved the once-in-a-lifetime achievement!

Muktak was breathing hard; his trunk was swaying.

'What a great honour for you, sir!' continued Sheru. 'There are many teachers in our land, but no mentor can claim to have achieved what you did through me! Now every teacher will look at you with envy and every junglezen will line up here to be under your charge.'

By then, Muktak was breathing very hard. He stomped his feet, swayed his body, and trumpeted in anger, 'That old fox! That old fox!'

Sheru was baffled, but he did not dare ask the

reason for Muktak's anger. He concluded that the high and mighty are all a bit loose in the head. So when he was asked by Muktak to follow him, Sheru tucked his tail between his legs and walked quietly behind him. It was hard to believe that it was the same lion who had raced through the forest like blazing fire moments ago.

The royal court was celebrating the taming of Sheru when Muktak gatecrashed. 'What is all this nonsense about Sheru becoming your entertainer? I demand an unconditional apology.'

If Muktak found confidence in the rightness of his demand, Kapi found confidence in numbers. Like any other weak administrator, he felt strong only in the presence of his cabinet, and he doled out all prize and punishment in their presence only. Kapi called it democracy, but his detractor called it hypocrisy.

'Junglezen Muktak, this is a State affair. You have no right to interfere in this.'

'Stop calling me Junglezen, you blighted clown. Your state affair is all rat poop, and you are only a bunch of selfish, cunning, and greedy rascals. I wonder if the world has ever seen a more self-serving bandit like you.'

'Mr Muktak! We have all along known that you are an anti-establishment rogue. If you are not satisfied with what we are doing, then why don't you just leave this holy land and find better opportunities in some circus? You can play football there and earn good fodder for your efforts.'

Muktak got so angry that he straightened his trunk horizontally and opened his mouth wide to take in more air to cool himself. The air flowing out of his trunk sounded like an approaching twister. The court was in mortal fear, but managed to find courage once again in numbers.

'You are trying to frighten us,' said a trembling Rig. Their fear of Muktak was genuine. 'We are not going to get cowed down by your antics.'

'I don't have to frighten a bunch of scheming cowards. In one step I can squash the whole bunch of you, and with my second step I can annihilate anyone who comes forward to support you. A third step will not even be needed.' Muktak told in a heavy voice.

This was followed by a deathly silence.

Having had his say, Muktak calmed down many notches. He breathed more softly and continued, 'But I will do nothing like that. From the day that my ancestors first appeared in this forest, we have been extra careful not to harm anyone, and not to let anyone come to harm when we are around. When we elephants first learn to talk, our mothers make us promise that the meaning, purpose, and essence of our existence is to protect our land and our people. I cannot break that solemn oath of my ancestors. I cannot break it even when I see you rascals destroying Sheru, the essence of this forest.'

Bhalu was a permanent fixture at the court. Although he was scared both of the lion and the elephant, he was not ready to accept these insults. He protested, 'Do not try to pass off your inability as greatness.'

Muktak turned towards him, 'Bhalu, you know well that even rhinos and hippos are no match for me when I am charged up. And you talk of inability! You have been eating from the hands of the monkey for far too long to have any dignity left. Even the little vitality that you had earlier is now gone.'

'If elephants can play football in a circus, what is wrong with Sheru carrying our Honourable Leader?'

'True. A monkey will always make a circus of all that is great in life.'

Rig realized from the words of Muktak that the royal court was completely safe. That gave him courage. He consoled Muktak, 'Noble sir! You have been our benefactor all along. You also promised to cooperate with us. We will not feel sorry if you kill us. But we will be devastated if you break your solemn promise of helping us in our work.'

'No need of your clever tricks, you fox. Save them for Magar, whose agent you have been in supplying the innocent animals as his meal.'

'That is a lie. You can't prove a thing,' howled a visibly agitated Rig.

'That you are asking for proof, itself proves your guilt. Your reactions would have been different if you were innocent. You can trick the masses, but you cannot fool one who knows the truth.'

By then, Muktak had crossed the peak of his anger; he was calm. Unlike the uncultured, a saint's anger does not increase with a shouting match.

He concluded, 'One last word to all of you who have been fiddling with the core of our folks. Each one of you is going to pay a nasty price for what you have done today. Empires fall when their strength is compromised, societies crumble when their ideals are compromised, and people are ruined when their essence is lost. You are guilty on all these counts. Now get ready for the vengeance of history, which will soon be upon you.'

There was nothing to be said. Kapi and others waited to see the end of all this.

Muktak continued in a resigned voice, 'I will leave you all to your fate. I will not wish you luck, folks, for there remains no more good luck for you. It is only a matter of time when our people, our society, and our empire will be brought to the brink of ruin by the folly of the fickle, the cunning, and the incompetent.'

Sheru could not understand why this heated exchange was taking place. The charm and grandeur of power was too tempting for him. He came near Muktak, held his trunk lovingly, and whispered, 'Sir, why are you getting all fired up? Now that I am in the corridors of power, you won't have to worry about a thing. I can get everything for you. Just prepare your wish list.'

Muktak replied in a drained voice, 'You are feeling proud for something which you should be ashamed for. What can I say?'

With those words he felt something sacred snapping inside him. He realized that he had lost Sheru. Probably forever. He hung his head and made a slow exit from the assembly. The tears in his eyes did not allow him speed.

The news of what happened at the court spread fast among the junglezens.

On his way back, Muktak was hit by a hard fruit that fell on his head. He moved his head to see a group of monkeys laughing at him. 'Hey short tail! Is it true that you ate up your own tail to fill up your belly?'

Muktak ignored them.

By then, the jackals had joined the fun. 'Is it true that God pulled your nose to this length because you are a greedy eater?'

Muktak ignored them too, and walked away with dignified steps to his dwelling place.

'Royal mount! How fast you are progressing, my dear dimwit!' Mr Python laughed. 'When I heard what was happening at the court, I had a desire to go and finish off those jokers. But our code strictly forbids us from interfering in the affairs of the leggies.'

Sheru had grown fond of Mr Python who did not scold him and was a repository of incidents, events, and stories of the forest. But the real reason behind it was Sheru's reluctance to learn the value-based wisdom of Muktak. Muktak always told Sheru what was really good for him while Mr Python told exactly what *appeared* good to him. This was a manifestation of the ageless battle between the noble and the pleasurable.

That day, as on some other occasions, Sheru did not like the way Mr Python was ridiculing him. He objected, 'Why do you ridicule me for something that is honourable?'

'Honour of being a monkey-carrier! Did you by any chance hit your head against a rock when you were born? Even if it was not so, you can accept it as true. That way whenever you are charged with stupidity, you can blame it on that proverbial rock. Why take the blame on oneself when the whole world is there to blame for your chinks?'

Sheru burned from inside, but kept quiet.

'I tell you, when I heard what the monkey was doing with you, I thought of breaking our code. I thought that I would visit the leggies, eat up the monkey as appetizer, and then have the jackal for a meal. But when I came to know of your wild ambitions, I withdrew.'

'Sir, you do get harsh. We are a free people with a dream. It is a matter of honour to be in the company of those who run the affairs of the State.'

'Forget it. I wonder if you will ever realize what you have been doing. Now listen. Your family has ruled over the forest for ages, so it is not in your blood to behave as a subordinate in the corridors of power. Sooner or later, you will make mistakes. So let me tell you some fundamental principles of service that I learnt from my ancestors.'

'That sounds interesting.'

Mr Python then instructed Sheru on organizational behaviour. 'Remember that every boss is necessarily a megalomaniac. He believes that the sun and the moon revolve around him, the climate changes occur according to his wish, and that he is the God in his set-up. That is exactly how I think of myself.'

'You sound humble, sir,' Sheru joked.

The python ignored the joke. 'So, be one-eyed, one-eared, and half-mouthed before him. Be blind to his faults, and see only his good deeds; be deaf to criticism against him, instead hear everything good said about him; and be mute – do not say anything negative about him, but sing his glories aloud.'

'You sound quite demanding.'

'Every boss is demanding. In fact, I demand much more. I also get rid of babblers, and those who offer unsolicited counsel. I think you know how I get rid of them?'

'Yes, sir. By putting them in your belly.'

Life in the forest has a cadence of its own. It has its own rhythms in accordance with which the animals eat, sleep, and mate – this again is a distant echo of nature's unbreakable rhythm, set by the cosmic order. This rhythm is best reflected in the change of seasons.

That year, when spring breezed in with its soft whispers and caresses, the forest felt it through the freshness of leaves and fragrance of flowers. The inhabitants felt a different kind of spirit welling up within them, which made them act in ways usually not seen at any other time of the year. Even Kaak, the jungle media, stopped his services for some days, and concentrated on collecting items for setting up a temporary home for his next generation.

As in previous years, the fragrance of the sweet smelling mohua flowers had started intoxicating everyone. Junglezens waited for the night when the annual party would be held and everyone would eat and enjoy the delicious flowers together. The practice had been going on since prehistoric times, and even Muktak joined this party. It was the only indulgence that he allowed himself. There were rumours that in his young days, he used to lose himself completely in the intoxicating dances that followed late into the night.

When the lion was alive, he used to inaugurate the party, taste one or two mohua flowers, and he then used to leave. He never participated in the revelry that went deep into the night. 'Never socialize with your unequals,' he used to tell his family.

But the forest now had a new way of life in which equality reigned.

Kapi believed in equality, but he also believed in selective equality on certain occasions. 'Junglezens! Let me first see for myself if it is safe and good for you to have the mohua party. I cannot risk your lives and honour, which is too precious,' he told the forest. He then organized his tribe of monkeys to have the party first. If anything remained after that, the junglezens could have their party.

'What a great sacrifice by our leader!' Barak, the goat philosophized.

'The rascal is off to his tricks,' Muktak sighed.

Even otherwise, he had no intentions of joining the party. Age had been catching up with him, and he strongly felt that there was no fool like an old fool who indulged in the activities of the young.

When the party began, Kapi ate a lot of flowers, and in no time lost control over his mind, speech, and action. Instead of bringing up the commoners to the level of the leader, the leader went down to the level of the commoners to wallow in the mud of collectivity.

The performer that he was, an inebriated Kapi got down to entertaining his tribe with his antics, acrobatics, and speeches. The trappings of power had kept him away from his performing art, which he had been missing terribly. Now there was his chance to come out of the isolation of power and enjoy his first love.

The crowd applauded his every move. There has never been a crowd that does not go wild at the buffoonery of its masters.

Kapi addressed them, 'My dear ones! It is said that a prophet is not worshipped in his own land. But brothers, I belong to you, and since you are applauding me, I must be the greatest of all prophets! He, he, he.'

'You know what! I can silence that silly Muktak with one kick of mine, but I have spared him because there is no one to shed tears for him.

'That Rig, you know, is a real crook. He had been sending the junglezens to the crocodile.'

The issue of Rig revived painful memories of the time when he, the leader, was being manipulated by the trickster. He felt low for a while, but the kick from mohua brightened his mood. He went back to his bragging.

As the royal mount, Sheru was the only outsider in the party. He watched the monkey-play with bemused eyes. Sheru thought, *even the high has his low!*

When the party was over late at night, Sheru carried his master back to his place. On the way, Kapi continued with his unplugged monologue on his worth, and the worthlessness of the entire world.

In the morning, Kapi felt embarrassed at what he had done the previous night in the presence of his attendant. To mend matters, he told Sheru, 'It was all a joke, you know. I was just acting to see how my people react to what I say.'

'Act? What act, sir? I suffer from night-time amnesia. I do not remember a thing that happens around me at night. Did something happen, sir?'

Kapi was not sure if Sheru was acting or not, so he let the matter go.

The memory of the previous night again gave him a high, and he issued the orders that it had been conclusively proved that partying was not good for the public, so anyone going to the mohua party would be banished from the land. From that time on, only the monkeys attended rave parties.

But what to do about the nervous energy of his folks which found expression during exciting seasons? Kapi thought over the issue, and started toying with the idea of a farm that would keep them engaged.

After his duty hour, Sheru went to meet the python and narrated to him the details. Mr Python was impressed.

'Character, Sheru, character! You have character, young one. Night-time amnesia indeed! You will go far Sheru.' Mr Python laughed aloud.

'Sir.'

'I wish I had committed ones like you in my service. The lot around me is simply worthless. In any case, only the worthless join the royal service.'

'I find your words humiliating.'

The python loved to listen to his own voice.

He continued. 'Once I had kept a smart-looking fellow to guard my place. That rascal started getting cosy with the females of my family. I had to then clean up the mess by eating him up.'

'Sir, how is it that all your problems get solved by your belly?'

'What a blessing it is to have a good appetite, Sheru. It sorts out many issues. No trace of the act remains, no word gets out, and my anger is also satisfied.'

'You can be gross.'

'There is more to it. My eating them up is all about synergy. Do you know what it is? It is when two things cooperate to produce a better performance. By eating up the incautious and the worthless, I create a tremendous amount of synergy. I am told that synergy is the latest trend in the city too where big houses gobble up the smaller ones.'

The clever can come up with explanation for the most trivial, Sheru concluded but kept silent.

Mr Python continued, 'I strongly advise you to stay careful about Lady Monkey and Lady Fox. Do not get too close to them.'

'Now that is a rotten one from you, sir! How can you even imagine such a preposterous thing?'

'Folks think that they are immune to charms till

they are exposed to it. Do not think yourself to be great till you walk out of the fire of temptations unscathed. Even the saintliness of the saints remains as long as they stay away from the snares of charm. Most saints start behaving like scorpion-stung monkeys once they get a taste of bewitchment. '

'Sir, you sure are a storehouse of wisdom,' joked Sheru.

'It is a pity that you are not the king of the forest. I have many tips about leadership too.'

'We have no kings, sir. We are all junglezens. We are all equal.'

'You know what? Although you do not really suffer from night-time amnesia, you do forget who you are – a kind of self-amnesia. That is one area where I cannot help you.'

'The Prophet is back! The Prophet is back!' Kaak was hawking the breaking news all over the forest.

Sheru was lazing in his lair and musing over his life. When he was young, he would use his thoughts only to imagine his future. But now as he was growing, he had plenty of encounters and experiences every day. This helped him dwell on memories and selective memories. 'Lucky me! What is good, is good for me and comes without any riders. I eat well, sleep well, and relax well. Some great teachers have imparted excellent education to me, and thanks to my great job in the corridors of power, I have all the right connections. Ah me!'

He mused further, 'I cannot be the leader because I do not have the numbers to back me up. But why regret over what one does not have?'

His musings were sharply interrupted by the news announced by the crow. He jumped up to find out what the matter was. Kaak informed him that Kurma, the tortoise, was back from his long sojourn. He was the prophet.

What kind of prophet can a tortoise be? Sheru wondered.

Kurma, the prophet, claimed to have seen more than three hundred springs. Even Muktak had heard from his grandmother that when she had been young, Kurma measured more than three metres from front to back, and looked like a mini hilltop.

The weak marvelled at his tough exterior, the strong praised his wisdom, and the old were wonderstruck at his long life. But he was best known for being a noble soul. Perfectly noble. Everyone thought that he could read minds, and could reach out to the needy even before they approached him. Many thought that he had psychic powers. Probably that was true.

The forest was Kurma's motherland, and hence highly sacred for him. He, however, rarely came to visit it, and there would be long stretches of absence in between his visits. When asked what he did during his absence, he narrated stories and adventures that sounded unbelievable. However, everyone believed him, loved him, and felt mesmerized by him.

Sheru decided to meet this wonderful being.

He started for the river where the prophet was then staying. On the way, he was stopped by Shuka, the parrot. 'You must be going to meet that old humbug. He is no prophet, I tell you. How can he be a prophet when he does not have eleven disciples, the mandatory number?'

Sheru retained respect for all his teachers. He said, 'You must be right, sir. I am going to find out why he does not have as many disciples if he is a prophet. I will come and report to you the details I gather, sir.'

When Sheru reached Kurma's place, folks had already assembled in good number. Young zens, curious as they were, went to watch the show and could be heard muttering 'Prophet! Indeed!'

Sheru reached to see a mini hilltop of a

creature, as silent and immobile as a dead buffalo, resting on the banks of the river. One look at Kurma's shell, and Sheru realized that not even a huge rock could crack it. 'Amazing! I wish I had something like this. But yes, that would affect my mobility.'

The noise of the gathering brought the sage out of his shell. His retractable limbs and neck stretched out of their safety to meet a bouquet of greetings and a barrage of questions.

'What is the secret of your survival, sir?' asked an old zen. He had hardly seen ten monsoons, and was already finding it difficult to carry his own body.

'We have heard that you are truly wise. Even wiser than Muktak, the elephant. What helped you achieve wisdom, sir?'

Sheru also had a question. 'What makes you so popular, so successful, sir?'

Kurma turned his neck in the direction of Sheru, and with a twinkle in his eyes, said, 'Withdrawal. Withdrawal. Withdrawal.'

The zens, particularly Sheru, stared at the sage, perplexed. After a pause, Kurma explained, 'My answer to all three questions is, withdrawal. Now go home and think. I can only give you the words; the understanding has to be your own.'

To everyone's surprise, Kurma, without another word, withdrew his limbs and neck inside his shell. Incommunicado!

After a short wait, bored junglezens started leaving. The young ones were the first to leave, the inquisitive were the next, and the lazy ones were the last to leave.

Sheru waited.

Something made Sheru feel that Kurma's words had been directed towards him, and that he would soon come out of his shell to speak to him once everyone had left. He was right. Kurma did come out when everyone left.

'I knew you would stay for me. I had deliberately withdrawn to get away from the flippant ones.'

'Thank you, sir.'

'I knew your father well. When I came to know of the developments here, I decided to come back and help my people. Of course, how can a globetrotter claim to have his own people? It is an oxymoron.' He laughed.

'Sir?'

'It is sad what is happening here. I am also sad about you.'

Sheru would tolerate anything, but not an attack on his beliefs; he was too passionate about 'equality' and 'community'. 'Sad? Why sad? I am proud to be a junglezen. I also hold a highly coveted position. What else does one want in life, sir? I may not have your long life, I may not have a hard shell like yours on my back, I may not have your popularity and following, but I do have my identity.'

'Let me answer your questions one at a time. Three questions were asked to me a while ago. I gave the same answer to all of them, "withdrawal". You know why? See, I have survived long because I can withdraw my limbs inside the safety of my shell. Nothing can harm me when I am inside my fort.'

'But what about human beings, sir? Can't they harm you?'

'Human beings? Ah! Do not bring them into our discussion. They are a different breed altogether. They are the only beings in this world who can kill, and keep killing even themselves. Not only that. They can kill, and they kill even their God. Poor God! He survives only because He is infinite.'

Sheru did not understand a word, but he nodded his head. After all, it is never good to reveal one's ignorance in the first meeting with someone.

'There have been occasions when I was trapped in the net cast by the fishermen,' continued Kurma.

'But I could cut through them and escape. Now I am careful enough to avoid them. It is good to come out of the trap, but it is better not to go near it. The wise never hover around a trap.'

Sheru had neither seen any net, nor any trap. He again nodded his head.

'The answer to the second question also was "withdrawal". When I was young, my folks taught me that this river was our home, our playground, and our ultimate resting place. But curiosity made me go beyond their words. I withdrew from my family, relatives, friends, and home. That is how I travelled through hundreds of rivers, and finally reached the ocean, and enjoyed its majesty.'

'So one has to go to the ocean to be great, is that so?'

Kurma ignored the interruption. 'Withdrawal freed me from my narrow existence. I prefer living in and around the ocean but occasionally, I remember my folks, and I come back to them to talk about the immensity of existence. But most of them do not believe me, and the few who believe me, shed tears in the name of their wife and children, and express their helplessness to enjoy the great.'

'They are right, sir. Even I would do the same if I had a family. Why should one leave the certain for the uncertain?'

'That exactly is the reason why you do not have wisdom. Wisdom comes from knowledge, knowledge comes through exposure, and exposure comes through withdrawal from the limits of existence.'

'Heavy stuff, sir.'

'Oh, but it is quite simple. See, you think yourself to be a unit that is separate from the world, which you think of as another larger unit. This reflects in your interaction with everyone – you bump into them like two solid balls crashing into each other. I, on the other hand, see myself as one with the universe. I exist, so all this exists; and all this exists, so I also exist. We are one and the same – infinite.'

'Much too heavy, sir!'

'Not at all. You have grown up hearing junk. That is why anything good appears heavy to you. Your problem is that you identify yourself as Sheru, but never as a lion ...'

'Sir, we are all junglezens now. It is a great advancement from the prehistoric mentalities.'

'The first step to wisdom lies in calling a lion, a lion. The second step is to believe that a lion is a lion. The third step is to realise that a lion is a lion. And the final step to wisdom lies in treating a lion as a lion.'

'Sir, may I come at some other time?'

'Sure, Mr Lion. But before that, you have to listen to the answer of the third question. After all, you were the one who asked that question.'

'I am sorry that I ever asked you that.'

Kurma ignored the reluctance. 'When you have power, the world will follow you like a dog. And when you are detached about that power, the world will adore you as a prophet. At present, you have neither power nor detachment. You only have a hollow desire to be adored. That will take you nowhere.'

'Sir, I am leaving.'

'Sure. Go and carry that joker on your back.' After a short pause, Kurma said prophetically, 'If you compromise your strength, you will only be left with weakness.'

Sheru had a twinkle in his eyes. He wanted to ask if Kurma had gone to the same school with Muktak, but Kurma stopped him with, 'It is good to know that others echo my thoughts.'

That flustered Sheru, who thought that Kurma could read his mind. He wanted to run away from there, but Kurma seemed to have fixed him to a spot.

Kurma continued, 'If you do not feel one with the commoners when you are young, then you have a stone for your heart. And when you want to be one with them even after you have grown up, then you have a stone for your head. Focus on your strength; focus on your individuality. That is the best way to serve others.'

Sheru did not want to hear all that. He bowed to take leave, and then walked away slowly. After a few steps, he broke into a run and vowed never to come back to this sacrilegious and seditious sage. Or, whatever he was.

Shuka is right. The fellow is only a humbug, concluded Sheru.

Kurma watched the fleeting figure of the young lion with bemused eyes. He smiled, and then jumped into the river to float in the free-flowing water.

The news of the prophet reached the royal court too.

Kapi had heard about sadhus and mahatmas during his city days. He had heard that these mendicants were good at revealing people's past and future. He had never believed in those stories, but he now thought of meeting the prophet to find out his future. He asked Sheru to accompany him to the tortoise, but Sheru politely refused. 'Sir, he is a humbug. He lectures on annoying topics, and most of the things that he says are incomprehensible. His words can even be hurtful.'

Sheru's words only made Kapi more curious, and one day he went all alone to meet Kurma. The private visit would also ensure that his linens were not washed in public.

Kurma welcomed Kapi. 'Do not hope that I will address you with high sounding titles like *king*, or *leader*. It would be a lie if I addressed you so, for you are nothing like that to me – me, the free. Free of pretensions and expectations.'

His words upset Kapi. He *was* the leader. He expected a minimum show of respect from others.

Kurma continued, 'Since you consider yourself a leader, you must struggle to be one. You cannot hold a position satisfactorily for long if you are not fit for it. So let me tell you what you must do to develop some qualities of a leader.'

Kapi interrupted, 'Mr Prophet, I am interested in knowing my future. Can you read the stars?'

'Why involve stars when anyone can predict the future of a failed leader? You are going to be hounded out of this place if you do not pay heed to what I say. You are fickle, indecisive, and wasteful.'

Kapi was agitated. 'Who told you all these lies? That cunning Rig? He has been spreading rumours about me.'

'It means that you should have the right assistants around you. I have seen kings coming to ruin because they had wrong assistants, or took decisions all alone, or because they consulted with too many. Remember that your subordinates will indulge in vices many times more than what you indulge in. They will practise only a fraction of all the good that you practise. So be careful about how you present yourself in public, and how you behave in private. Unless you are self-disciplined, there is no possibility of your assistants behaving in a disciplined manner.'

It was all boring for the fickle. Kapi had come with the hope to hear about himself – his glorious present and his brilliant future. And here was this old nut! Dishing out the unpalatable.

Kurma looked into the monkey's eyes and said, 'Take care of the underprivileged. If pained, their tears will ruin you in this life and the next. Never indulge in favouritism. This particular vice has been at the root of the collapse of every good institution.'

'May I leave, Mister?' The monkey had now

begun to insult him. He left Kurma without even saying goodbye.

Kurma laughed. 'This fellow will surely ruin the land of my birth. He has every defect that a leader must not have.'

He then jumped into the river to float effortlessly – to float was to experience victory, mastery, freedom, and joy. Mukti.

V

The Farm

'This is the one great thing to remember, it has been the one great lesson I have been taught in my life; strength, it says, strength, O man, be not weak.'

– Swami Vivekananda

Since the day he had come to the forest, Kapi had been unhappy about eating what the forest had to provide. 'Not at all good for a city-trained stomach,' he told himself. There also was the issue of keeping the nervous energy of the excitable under check. All this fructified in the idea of farming. To announce his great step, he called a meeting.

The forest folks were by then accustomed to being called for meetings where Kapi loved to act out the comical aspect of power. With his natural talent to back him up, he never had difficulty convincing the crowd. The bigger the lies, the more convincing he sounded.

Kapi raised a new slogan. 'To farming! To farming!' He talked about the importance of the cultured habits, calorie, cholesterol, and height-weight ratio. Those who did not like the idea were asked to leave the forest, which no one dared to do.

The jungle echoed 'To farming! To farming!'

Muktak was left out of the grand operation. 'He is anti-establishment,' was the standard comment by the authorities for leaving him out of all their activities. That suited well with Muktak too.

Rig was made the chief supervisor of production, distribution, and storage. The pigs were given charge of looking after the daily running of the farms.

Thanks to the zeal of the young, the farming-idea was a grand success. This encouraged Kapi to make a tour of inspection of the farm. He mounted Sheru and headed towards the farm. Sheru was careful not to take the route where Mr Python lay in wait for the lazy.

It was a coincidence that Hiru, the deer, was also out on some errand, and he too avoided the route on which the predator lay. That is how the old friends crossed paths.

Sheru had not seen Hiru since their school days, but he had never forgotten him for a day.

'*Hiru*!' Sheru let out a loud cry on seeing his old mate, and ran towards him at full speed. Emotions made him forget that he was on royal duty.

Sheru's loud call was the roar of a lion. All those who heard it were terrified. Hiru too was scared. He ran for his dear life. The racial memory of the deer concerning roars of a lion gave speed to his legs.

Sheru could not understand why his friend was running like that. To reach his friend, he focussed all his strength on his legs, and as he ran, he shouted, 'Wait Hiru, wait.' His speed made him look like a stick of fire, while the fresh mane on his shoulders appeared like the flames of that burning stick. The forest trembled with fright.

Kapi was not accustomed to this kind of power. He could not maintain his hold on a speeding Sheru, and so he jumped up to catch hold of a branch for safety. Sheru did not even notice the absence of his master from his back.

With great difficulty, Sheru cornered his old friend and said, 'Hello! How have you been doing? I wonder if you even remember me!'

The flight for life had made Hiru pant excessively. When he realized that there was no imminent danger of death, his panting subsided. He looked deeply at Sheru and said, 'Now that you remind me, weren't we in that stupid school together? Probably.'

Sheru felt hurt at the indifference. 'Yes, that is true. How nice to see you again. Now that we are grown up, and now that destiny has brought us face to face, we can be friends again. I will get you a nice job at the royal court.'

By then the deer's composure had fully returned. He mocked, 'How great it would be to play nanny to the monkey's children! Mister, I will appreciate if our paths do not cross again. I have heard stories about you. Aren't you the mount of that monkey?'

'You mean Mr Leader.'

'Call him by whatever name, he will remain an empty-headed monkey. And, we have also heard that you walk behind that cunning fox with your tail tucked between your legs. Fah! You have no power. No honour. No competence.'

'Your words are harsh,' Sheru said in a low voice.

'You can kill me for that. But that is the truth, Sheru. Because I worked hard, I am skilled. I can run faster than anyone in the forest. I can fend for myself in safety and also in danger, whereas you have lost your very basics. You have nothing left inside you. You are a rotten piece of wood. Leave alone being friends with you, I won't even like to be seen with you – a stuffed lion. I now request you to step aside and make way for my passage.'

Hiru did not wait for a response and left.

The reality check made Sheru collapse where he was standing. His legs went rubbery, hands trembled, heart pounded, mouth was parched, skin went wet, body was aflame, and head reeled. Tears streamed down his cheek to soothe him.

It took time for Sheru to gain enough strength

to get up and walk back to Kapi's place, where he found the royal court waiting for him.

'You should be banished from the forest for behaving in such an undignified way. You even put Mr Leader's life under grave risk.' The court was firm in its pronouncement.

After the shabby treatment by Hiru, the words of the elders sounded like sweet nothing to Sheru. But again, he had no desire to leave the forest.

'Forgive me, sir! It was my first mistake.'

'We have overlooked lots of your mistakes in the past.'

Sheru could not remember any past misdemeanour of his. 'But why argue with the powerful,' he thought, and apologized with bowed head. 'Honoured sirs! I will die if I am banished from here. Give me one chance. Just one chance, sir.'

But the court did not relent.

Sheru then turned towards Dholu, 'Sir, you have been my honoured teacher.'

'When I was your teacher, it was different. Now I am a responsible and respected member of the board. Do not expect me to take sides,' said Dholu. Like any other incapable fellow in power, he did not have the courage to stand up against the powerful in favour of the beaten.

Sheru hung his head.

'A minute, please!' It was Kurma, the tortoise. It seemed as if he had materialized from nowhere. This surprised everyone at the court, though they all knew that he had such powers.

The forest folks were of the opinion that Kurma had special powers that enabled him to appear and disappear at will. But this was not true. Kurma had mastered silence – the way Muktak had mastered stillness. Muktak could focus all his strength on any part of his body with his stillness. This gave him invincible strength. Kurma, on the other hand, was the master of silence. This gave him complete control over his body and also over his mind. Because of his mental stillness, he could become aware of others' thoughts even before they came to their conscious level. Kurma would then take the shortest path through land, river, mountain, valley, and desert to reach the needy.

'A minute, please!' Kurma repeated.

'Yes?' Kapi demanded. He remembered how Kurma had lectured him on leadership qualities. He did not want that to be repeated in front of his subordinates.

'It will be wrong on your part to banish Sheru from the forest. Its consequences will be severe for all of you.'

'Save your sermons for the naive,' said Kapi

with annoyance. As he uttered the words, he picked up a stone and threw it at Kurma.

'Stone, ah! Cast not stones at what you can't break.'

Kapi looked foolishly at Kurma.

Had the fear of the powerful not been there, the council would have laughed at the vague attempt of Kapi. Everyone knew that Kurma's shell was unbreakable, and that he was beyond death and injury caused by ordinary folks.

'The last time we met, I did not tell you one important thing about leadership. It is that when you punish someone, your heart should also cry like the mother whose child is being punished. Can you do that? If not, then you are not fit to lead.'

Kapi seethed in fury at the insult.

'Kapi, you are a monkey, and you can never get out of your racial defects. You will always be vain, fickle, and revengeful. As a well-wisher of all, I caution you that it will be wrong for you to banish Sheru from his rightful place in the forest.'

The words of Kurma made no impression on him. He was a performer who listened only to a director; he was not a learner who could listen to a master.

The court, however, realized the potential of this case. Quick whispers and glances were exchanged, and it became clear to all that there could be serious reprisals if Sheru was harmed. Muktak and Python could even attack them, and annihilate them forever.

'A banished Sheru would be more dangerous than a punished Sheru,' the court whispered. They then tried to work out a way to find an honourable exit from the impasse.

The court doled out its unanimous verdict. 'Banished from the royal court. To work at the farm.'

Sheru gratefully agreed to that. Anything was acceptable to him as long as he was not thrown out of the forest. So he thanked the court profusely for its kindness.

Kurma had disappeared by then. No one had seen him go.

'Wonderful! Wonderful! Lettuce farm! His Majesty working on a lettuce farm! My, my!' Mr Python laughed and rolled on the ground. He must have been hungry, otherwise his stomach would have split by his loud rolling and laughing.

'You embarrass me, sir,' said Sheru with dignity.

'I feel happy that I am friends with you. I would have missed out on the laughter of my life otherwise. A lion working in a lettuce farm! My, my!'

'Sir, we are all junglezens.'

Mr Python laughed more, 'Yes, yes. I forgot that you are the committed fool of the forest.'

Sheru had grown up with the ideals of junglezen. He could not think of anything else in his life. So he ignored the barbs of the wise, and said, 'It is wrong of you to ridicule our efforts, sir. Distribution of labour and discipline demand that we take up any work that comes our way. There is no high or low work in an ideal set-up.'

'Misery makes us philosophers – never before did the statement seem more true. The best of Sheru is coming out when he is down! Good, good. I must tell my family all about this.'

Sheru choked on his own emotions.

Mr Python continued, 'It is sad for me to see the master become the lowly servant. I can, however, tell you the fundamentals of becoming successful at work. Who knows? You may even come out of your mess by achieving perfection in your work.'

'Sir.'

'Take care of the micro, and you will be the master of the macro.'

'Sir.'

'Do not go for big acts till you realize the truth of inequality in life. Every society is a parasite on the big doers. The bigger your work, the greater will be the number of parasites clinging to you till you die.

'Parasite?'

'Yes, parasite. There never was a society that did not talk of equality, but in reality, was entrenched in harsh inequality. That is the only way to make the foolish work for the intelligent. If you know this, you will realize that every great worker is essentially a great fool who ends up working endlessly for others.'

'Sir!'

'Look, only the truly great like me have the courage to declare inequality as the law of life. For the rest, words like "commitment" and "service" are mere masks to exploit the gullible,' continued Mr Python. 'That is how every "good" system sucks and then destroys great many lives. The better the system, the more parasitical it is, and the more lives it destroys.'

'Sir, you can be truly vitriolic.'

'Straightforwardness is my strength. Just see, even my belly is straight!'

Sheru remained silent.

'Till now you were in the royal service, so

you were immune to certain kinds of exposure. But now that you will be working alongside the commoners, you need to learn certain things.'

'I am a great learner, sir. In my days, I had a good number of teachers.'

Mr Python knew all about Sheru's teachers, so he ignored that and said, 'The farms are run by the greedy pigs. The greedy like to do many things at the same time. You be careful about it, and stay away from multitasking.'

'Why Sir?'

'The pigs are supervised by the cunning foxes. The cunning are always ambitious and scheming. So be careful not to be influenced by their traits.'

'You can be insulting, sir. How can you even imagine that I would become wily?'

'As your well-wisher, I am only cautioning you. I am not being personal; I am just speaking generally.'

'Sir.'

'The king influences his subjects. The monkey being your head, there is the fear that you too may become fickle and indecisive like him. So be careful, and make a vow to complete what you have undertaken.'

'Even otherwise I do that. All my teachers have been proud of me.'

'Above all, harmonize your thoughts, words, and actions. Your thoughts lead you into action, and your action shapes your personality. Your future is determined by what you believe and how you act in the present. I have seen many lives being ruined because of a lack of coordination between the two.'

Sheru thanked Mr Python for his words of wisdom. 'I will strive to bring you satisfaction, sir.'

'Nothing will satisfy me till you start roaring and be what you are. Nothing will make me more happy than to see you stop making efforts to be what you are not. Nothing will give me greater joy than to see you established in your true nature.'

'Let us not try to kill what is already dead.' Sheru said, and left.

Mr Python was rarely troubled by what happened around him. But the Sheru affair was disturbing him deeply. He sighed, 'Lion in a lettuce farm, ah!' He thought for some time and then decided to go and visit Kurma. He climbed down from the tree and slithered towards the river.

'Hello Mr Big Neck!' Mr Python greeted Kurma. 'Be not annoyed with my informality. I can always take liberty with you. After all, we are both reptiles. We are equals.'

'You can take liberty with anyone in this world, Mr Big Belly,' Kurma laughed. 'But we are not equals. You live only for yourself, while I live for others.'

'When you live for others, then also you live only for yourself. After all, you consider others too as yourself only.'

'The difference lies in universality. Your happiness is limited to your being happy, but my happiness is unlimited.'

Before Mr Python could say something clever, he saw Muktak approaching them. That made everyone happy. There were greetings all around, and then the python laughingly said, 'In the regime of long tail, there is no relevance left for long tusk, or long neck. Only long belly manages to save his dignity.' His whole belly shook with laughter – the sign of genuineness.

'Make no mistakes there,' replied Kurma. 'Muktak and I will always be relevant for all. Other kinds of dazzle will come and go.'

Muktak commented sadly, 'We tried so much to make Sheru realize what he truly is, but every effort was in vain.'

Kurma smiled and said, 'Your efforts will not go in vain. No idea, howsoever insignificant, ever gets lost. It manifests when its time comes.'

'By then everything will be over.'

'That is where you and I differ, Muktak. You give too much value to what you perceive, but I give value only to existence in its entirety. You get emotionally charged despite all your knowledge, while I am able to stay detached. Friend, nothing gets lost, nothing gets destroyed. At the worst, things change their external form only.'

Mr Python said, 'Wait, wait. Do you people always talk like this? Stop it and come down to the ground. My head is churning.'

'Ah!' Kurma smiled.

Mr Python said, 'One thing is there. Where you two failed, I succeeded. I could at least teach Sheru the ways of the world. I am greater than you two wise fellows put together.'

'That is what every materialist thinks, sir. Materialism has its own place in life. It is only the simpletons who think it to be the ultimate.'

'You are getting personal. I think I should leave. Also, I am quite hungry.'

'It was just a general statement and not a personal attack, brother. But yes, take your leave. Bon appétit!'

After the python had left, Kurma told Muktak, 'Unlike me, you belong to this forest. Even when everyone goes against you, or stays indifferent to you, you will have to protect this land in crisis. Let the foolish enjoy their fortune; the wise have to stay prepared for the unfortunate.'

Kurma then jumped into the river for his free float, and was soon lost in deep contemplation.

Sheru was happy at the farm.

The wild nature had been tamed in the confines of plots of the farm to yield fruits and vegetables. 'I wonder how I had missed this. Nothing like working for the masses. This is the place where I can practise good of all and growth of all.'

Like all the hard working folks, junglezens at the farm were noble at heart. The feeling of being a community reigned supreme. Tears of one were the tears of all, and the profit of one was the profit of all. Sheru did not take long to become one with this community.

The vacuum in Sheru's life made him crave for a personal company. So when he met Jebo, the rabbit, he wondered how he had missed meeting this beauty of creation all his life. Like any other lonely fellow, he found everything divine about his companion, howsoever unworthy he might have been.

'Junglezen Jebo, I am charmed by your pure

whiteness. Your heart too must be as pure. And what pearly eyes you have! Divine!'

Sheru was also fascinated by the way timid Jebo ran – now running, now stopping, now linear, now zigzag. Folks found it funny to see Sheru imitate that style, but he found it impressive. *Muktak would have said that everyone apes in the kingdom of the ape. How foolish of him! This is the way all of us should walk*, thought Sheru. *What grace!* Sheru was one day practising the 'graceful gait' when he heard the now familiar 'A minute please!'. It was Kurma. It is said that an ordinary teacher instructs and leaves his disciple, but a great teacher strives to make his disciple see reason by pushing him to his limits. Kurma was a great teacher. He was not giving up on Sheru.

Sheru cursed his luck. He knew that he was in for a long talk. To compensate, he replied, 'Your minute never ends in a minute.'

'No meaningful talk ever takes more than a minute. It is the explanation of that point to the dull that takes hours.' Kurma laughed and continued, 'Sheru, if you do not act according to your higher nature, nature will pull you down lower and lower.'

Sheru ignored the talk and chose to remain silent.

'The goal of life is to be universal. Confuse this not with the collective, for the journey from the collective to the universal can be made only by possessing a strong sense of individuality. If you have no individuality, you will end up with the collective. As I told you in our first meeting, I was one with the collective of my people when I was young. But when I started working on my strength, I outgrew my own folks to become universal. Now I belong to every water, every land, and every people. If my folks are today proud of me, it is not because of my collective existence, but because of my universality.'

'Look, sir, you all talk to me about this and that nature, whereas our leader talks about community. Tell me, why should I believe your words over his?'

'Ah, that is simple. The teaching that brings out more of your universality, is the correct teaching. Look at that bird collecting grains,' Kurma pointed at a nearby bird, and continued, 'It can walk on its two legs; it can also fly. If a teacher asks him only to use his legs, then the rule of universality will be violated. By learning to fly, the bird becomes airborne, which has more universality than it being mere earthbound.'

'Maybe. But why should I believe that universality is better? It is only your words.'

It does not happen every day that a prophet is lost for words. But that was the day the prophet had to pause for a proper reply to Sheru. That broke the magnetic bond that had kept Sheru fixed to a spot. He ran away.

Kurma smiled, 'A stubborn one can beat the wise hollow.'

The bison, who had been happy at the lion's death, had steadfastly refused to be under the new rule. 'I did not care for the lion, and you expect me to be pushed around by a monkey!' he would say to those who tried to impress him with the idea of junglezen.

When the farm grew to a considerable size, the bison's attention was drawn to it. The green meadows and orchards attracted him, and he became an admirer of the idea of junglezen. 'Fantastic! They are great workers. Now I won't have to forage for food. I can just walk up and have my fill from the farm.'

The workers at the farm did not like it when the bison came to eat their produce regularly. They went and complained at the royal court.

Kapi came with his council to see the losses, and after assessment asked Bhalu to take steps. The obedient Bhalu went to the bison and asked him to stop trespassing. In reply, the bison charged at him ferociously. The security chief had to make a bloody retreat.

The council was now confused. What to do with rogue elements?

Rig then whispered something into the ears of Kapi, who looked at Sheru and called him.

'How have you been keeping, Sheru? We miss you badly. You are not at the royal court, but does that mean you will throw us out of your heart?' asked Kapi and gave a bright smile.

Sheru choked with emotion. He felt like crying and embracing his old master. However, he checked himself because of the crowd.

Kapi continued, 'Sheru, the bison has to be tamed. You alone can do it. Go and silence him.'

Sheru had been so moved by the kind words of Kapi that he did not care for anything else. He ran towards the farm and headed straight to where the bison stayed. Jebo tried to stop him, but he replied, 'Worry not. My teachers have trained me well. Just see what I can do.'

Sheru went near the bison's lodgings, and touched a nearby tree for good luck, remembering how the squirrel had taught him to touch wood. He then challenged the bison, 'Junglezen bison! I am counting up to eleven, the divine number. I ask you to surrender by then, or else ...'

'Really?' asked the bison and charged at Sheru, who was busy counting. Before he could reach the number eleven, he was scooped up on the horns by the bison and thrown a long distance away.

Sheru cursed his fate for not being able to count till eleven in time, and limped back to the farm, where everyone was waiting.

Seeing the plight of Sheru, Kapi laughed, 'I knew you were a worthless fellow. I wonder what good this dim-witted Rig saw in you. I could have wound up that bison in my tail and thrown him in the river. But as a considerate leader, I cannot do that.'

'I am sorry sir.' Sheru said.

Jebo, the rabbit, who had witnessed the whole episode, was angry. He screamed at Sheru, 'Sorry for what? These powerful ones have destroyed your power by keeping you in the dark. And now they expect you to fight. I tell you, Sheru, even I have more strength than you.'

Sheru was embarrassed by his friend's outburst, and apologized to the council. Jebo continued with his rants till the council had left.

Before leaving, Kapi told Sheru, 'You are becoming a real misfit. I advise you to pay attention to the farm work. Otherwise, you may have to leave the forest.'

That was enough for Sheru. He began to work more eagerly at the farm. Soon the production was up despite the losses caused by the bison.

But there were other looters too.

The farms were under the supervision of the pig, who sat under a tree and ordered the workers around. Sheru found that impressive. 'What great responsibility! It requires brains to run this kind of a show.'

Jebo objected, 'It only requires laziness to go higher up in power structure. The lazier you are, the higher you are pushed by the efforts of the active ones.'

'Fantastic! What understanding you have! Much better than Mr Python, and maybe even better than Mr Muktak.' Sheru admired Jebo so much that he needed flimsiest of reasons to appreciate him.

One day, when these two were taking a walk and discussing the weather, they discovered a tunnel running out of the farm. Curiosity led them to explore it. To their surprise, they found that it led to a store where a lot of farm products were carted away by the pig himself. Sheru caught him red-handed.

'Sacrilege! This is sacrilege. How can you, the head of farm hands, indulge in such muck?' Sheru screamed. He did not realize that pigs lived in and loved muck – both physical and social.

Caught in the act, the pig was startled. To cover up his deed he offered Sheru a share of his loot. 'Keep quiet and take as much as you want. It will work to the satisfaction of all.'

Sheru was scandalized. He refused the offer, and threatened to inform all. The threat galvanized the pig into action. He started squealing and screaming loudly to call his mates, 'Thieves! Thieves!'

Junglezens came running to see what the matter was. The pig explained that Sheru was stealing farm products in connivance with Jebo, who was an expert tunnel-maker. 'From the day that Junglezen Sheru has been here, I have smelled trouble. He is not a good fellow. Today, I unearthed what was below the earth. He was also discussing with Jebo about rebelling against our leaders.'

The words of the innocent drowned under the noise of the guilty. The royal court was hurriedly informed about the incident. Kapi and Rig soon reached the scene of the crime. Both of them were deep into theft, and were now worried about possible exposure. When they found that the pig had not squealed on them, Kapi became bold, and stood up to address the crowd.

'Junglezens! I always feel envious of you folks working for the good of all, growth of all. There have many occasions when I have felt like resigning from my post to work along with you.'

The performer paused for the effect. Of course, there was loud clapping.

'It breaks my heart to see how our two brothers are wrecking all that is sacred to us, particularly to me, your humble servant.' Kapi said, knowing well that humility was not his virtue. But that is what public speaking is all about; you must never tell the truth. Stick to what pleases the crowd. Their weak memory and weaker intelligence will be okay with everything.

'A minute please!' Kurma had appeared amidst them mysteriously.

Kapi and Rig felt uncomfortable. Their past encounters with the tortoise had not gone well.

Kurma began, 'A leader protects the noble and punishes the wicked. When it becomes the opposite, know then that the system is about to collapse.'

'You want us to forgive the culprits?' Kapi raised his voice.

Kurma looked intensely at Kapi. The look seemed to reveal the truth about the theft. After a moment he said, 'No. Not at all. Never forgive the guilty, even if it be his first mistake. The system will collapse if you do so. The wicked will think that they can get away with their misdemeanours the way the first timers got away. But never punish the innocent. So release Sheru.'

'You are accusing us of miscarriage of justice?'

'Yes.'

'You are going too far. This time we will not spare you.' Having said this, Kapi turned towards the crowd and said, 'Finish off this senile. Destroy him. I order you.'

No one stirred.

Kapi may have been the ruler of their lives, but the forest folks treated Kurma as sacred – much higher than the mundane.

Kurma smiled, 'If I want, I can turn the crowd on you, but I will not do that. I will not interfere in the affairs of the State. I just ask that you release Sheru.'

'Okay, okay. Look, Sheru. Do not keep bad company, and do not indulge in bad acts. Good boy then,' said Kapi, and left the place with Rig.

With nothing exciting left to witness, the crowd too went away. Only an angry Sheru and a calm Kurma were left.

Kurma soothed Sheru, 'Never expect anything from the powerful. They are always too self-centred to be considerate.'

Sheru was livid, 'Sir, it is sheer miscarriage of justice. At least our honourable leader should have listened to what I had to say.'

'Justice, ah! Justice, righteousness, values – these are all defined by the folks in power. Today, the power lies with Kapi. So whatever he says, that alone will be justice and right. Power is the only virtue in the world.'

'I think I should start a rebellion.'

Kurma laughed. He laughed so much that he could not utter a word. He simply jumped into the river, and bubbles of air released due to his laughter rose to the surface of the water.

Annoyed by Kurma's laughter, Sheru went to meet Mr Python. He took Jebo along with him. Once there, Jebo refused to go near the python. 'Safety lies in distance,' he said.

'Fantastic! This feather ball is your latest polestar. Fantastic! But he would look much better inside my belly.' Mr Python joked.

'You're truly crude. Very crude,' said Sheru. He,

however, had come with a purpose, so he narrated all that had happened at the farm.

'Wonderful! A thieving lion you are now! Wonderful. Are you done with this junglezen business?'

'What are you saying? Junglezen is an idea, and an idea never gets corrupted by the corrupt.' Sheru overlooked the fact that a moment ago, he had been talking about rebellion with Kurma.

'Your new friend has turned you into a thinker. Now look, the pig is not wrong. Honesty is lack of opportunity. Those who claim to be honest are in reality only weaklings.'

'You are truly crude, sir.'

'Not at all. Only those who are masters of their world can afford to be honest. You can be honest only if you have everything, or, if you give up everything. Till then, honesty is a mere word. It will leave you at the first opportune moment.'

'Sounds interesting.'

'Look at me. I am honest because everything of the reptile world belongs to me. The pig has to loot because not everything in the forest belongs to him. Also, why blame him alone? The corruption goes right up to Kapi. The hands of your leaders are as black as the hands of your boss.'

Sheru was now confused. He did not want to

believe Mr Python, and yet this master had never been wrong.

Seeing Sheru lost in his thoughts, Mr Python slowly extended his body towards Jebo, but the alert rabbit scampered away to safety with a scream.

Sheru was angry. 'Sir, an attack on a friend of mine is an attack on me.'

'You have immunity from my attacks. That does not mean that every rabbit, squirrel, and goat with whom you move will have immunity.'

'You are a disgusting gobbler. I should have never come to you. Bye.'

Sheru did not wait to hear Mr Python's response.

Once back, he was scolded severely by Jebo for keeping evil company. 'It is either me, or him,' demanded the terrified.

'Fear not, my friend. I will give up the world to be with you. I owe my life and happiness to you.'

Thus, Sheru continued working at the farm. Theft or no theft – he had to work for the good of all, growth of all. *Let Jebo be with me, and I will conquer the world*, Sheru would tell himself, without realizing that with a weakling for company, he could only be the conquered, and never the conqueror.

VI

The Finale

'Tat tvam asi – You are that supreme Reality'

– Chhandogya Upanishad

Life for Kapi and Rig had been like a never-ending spring – beautiful, powerful, and intoxicating. There were occasional hiccups, but they were ignored as professional hazards. But the danger that they now faced was life-threatening. Magar had called the duo for a serious and secret meeting.

'Power demands price. What do you say?'

'Sir.'

'Let us not go over it again.'

'Yes, sir.'

'My health has been deteriorating from the day that silly goat and the stupid cub came to the river. I have been somehow surviving on fishes. Not good for the delicate linings of my stomach.'

'Sorry, sir. That was a nasty episode. Even we could manage to survive only with great strategy. Unfortunately, the animals have become alert about going to the river when we order them to do so.'

'But how does it matter to me? You decide whether or not you want to stay in power.'

'Sir, we have started a big farm that produces

plenty of banana, lettuce, and cabbages. We have kept a modest supply safe from the public gaze. We will be grateful if you accept the whole thing as a humble gift from us.'

'Banana, lettuce, cabbages – fah! Greens are meant for the weak in head. You want my grey matter to be affected like my stomach linings? You are real conspirators. You are fit only for my belly.'

'We are extremely sorry, sir.'

'Now listen. Your own folks have been enjoying the by-products of royal power for a long time. I was watching them and found that each one of them is looking plump. Soon, they might need dieting to be able to walk properly. You have been serving yourselves well.'

The defensive ones did not comment.

'Power demands price and you have no choice but to pay it. Send one from your tribes every day to me. I will try and manage with a limited change of taste. There is no reason why your family and relatives should not make a small sacrifice for keeping you in power.'

'Sir, be not so cruel with us. One lives and labours for one's family and relatives. Take away all that we have collected from the farm, and spare us.'

'Power demands price. Pay if you want power

or get ready to hand it over to more deserving ones, like Sheru or Muktak.'

The very thought of Sheru or Muktak in power terrified the duo. They quaked. Yes, power was exacting its price.

'A minute please.' It was Kurma. He had mysteriously appeared in front of them. He said, 'When the fickle, the cunning, and the vile are together, it must be a deadly project.'

'Are you suggesting that we are into some kind of conspiracy?'

'I am not suggesting anything,' Kurma smiled. 'I am asserting that you are dangerous conspirators. I am also advising you to change your ways, else there will be a lot of bloodshed in this sacred land.'

'Do not try to threaten me.' Magar's tone was menacing as he advanced towards the tortoise.

Kurma laughed, 'I am entering my shell, and I promise to stay put so that I can enjoy your conversation.'

There was nothing that the trio could do about Kurma. Nor could they now make plans to satisfy Magar. The meeting had to end.

Before parting, Magar hissed, 'Beware of the fury of the patient.'

Later, Kapi and Rig made serious attempts to

resolve the conflict with Magar, but there was no way out of the piquant situation.

The wolves were persuaded by Magar that the forest was unprotected, and that the lion was working on a lettuce farm.

'Lion in a lettuce farm? It sounds like some kind of a joke.'

'Yes. The royal court is a pack of jokers.'

This gladdened the wolves. There were many scores to settle with the forest folks. Everyone planned to have his own share of revenge and loot.

The wolf army arrived well prepared to take over the unguarded. However, remembering their previous encounter, the commander took extra precautions this time. After entering the forest boundary, it gave out a low howl to indicate its intentions, and wait for the reaction.

Hiru, the deer, was the first to hear the low howl of attack. Terrified, he ran through the forest screaming, 'Run! Run! There is an attack. Wolves! Wolves!'

The screams of Hiru were picked up by Kaak. Startled, he started cawing in a frenzy and spread the news. His grating voice became so annoying to the aerofolks that once again he was accosted by the mynah, 'How does it matter who becomes the king? Nothing is going to change for you and me. You will get your garbage, and I will get my grains. So shut up.'

Kaak shut up. But the news of the attack, like any other good or bad news, had reached every corner of the forest by then.

It had been a long time since the junglezens had heard any roar or angry howl. The new generation did not even know that such things existed. Since birth, they had only heard the timid calls of the passive. So the sudden knock of danger froze their lungs, and also their wits.

The monkeys were the first to react. Kapi, along with his troupe, took the tree route to reach the river bank. He knew that even if he was captured by the city folk, he would get enough nuts for the remaining days of his life.

The jackals took the tunnel route to safety. 'If we survive, we should be able to hunt at nights,' they consoled themselves.

The easy food, and the power over the weak, had taken all fight out of Bhalu, the bear. He also ran towards the river shouting, 'Even if I am captured, I will be able to meet my brothers. There is always a bright side to everything.'

Dholu did not want to repeat the mistake of last time. He believed the fact that there was an attack. He ran straight towards the river. 'Let this crisis blow over. Something will work out in our favour.'

'Danger here, danger there. Let us not lose hope.' Barak, the goat philosophized, and ran with the fleeing animals towards the river.

The squirrels lost no time in taking to the trees, 'Hit the wood! Hit the wood! Brothers! Many of us will have to die to fill the belly of one brute. On your own! On your own!'

Some elderly members of the forest, who were not good with their legs, remembered Muktak, and went to plead with him to save the forest and its folks.

'Oh! Where are our leaders?' Muktak asked after he heard the details of the attack.

'Escaped. Every leader has escaped. Sir, there is no time. Save us.'

'Where is Sheru?'

The animals hung their head in embarrassment, 'At the lettuce farm, sir.'

'Lettuce farm? What is he doing there?'

'He is deep into lettuce farming with his friends. "Nothing like lettuce farming" he claims, and also persuades others to join it.'

'A lion in a lettuce farm! Indeed!'

Muktak thought for a moment, and then putting aside all his accumulated piques, he hurried to meet Sheru.

Sheru had missed the news of the attack. He was busy watering the lettuce plants with Jebo, the rabbit.

Muktak informed Sheru of the developments and asked him to accompany him, 'You are a lion. You are the essence and strength of the forest. Now get up and fight the wolves.'

'Our leaders! Where are they? Where is everybody else?' asked Sheru.

'Cowards! They have all run away to the river. Fools! They will soon be on dinner tables or in circus rings.'

'You mean to say that they are all safe from the wolves.'

'Yes.'

'What are we waiting for then? Come, let us forget our past differences, and run to join the crowd before it is too late. I assure you that I will be by your side in this calamity.'

'*What!* You are a lion. You cannot run away like that.'

'You are still holding on to your foolish ancient beliefs. There is nothing called a lion. There is only junglezen. I am proud to be Junglezen Sheru.'

Jebo did not wait to hear anything further. He started running towards the river with all his strength.

Sheru was startled, 'Where are you going, Jebo? Wait for me.'

A hurrying Jebo replied, 'Company lasts only till we are safe. During danger, safety lies in numbers. You can face the danger if you wish.'

'Wait, wait! Do not leave me like this in my hour of need. I am also coming with you.' Having said this, he wished Muktak a quick goodbye and dashed after Jebo. He ran as if his tail was on fire.

Muktak trumpeted, 'SHERU! COME BACK. YOU ARE A LION.'

Sheru neither listened, nor did he care to listen what this old master had to say. He ran and ran.

The wolves watched in disbelief how the lion was running away from them. 'Never heard of a lion running away like a commoner.'

'He must have got his priorities wrong in life,' said an elderly wolf.

'We can reign supreme in this forest for any length of time without shedding a drop of blood. All blood can now go inside our bellies.'

Muktak trumpeted helplessly, 'SHERU! COME BACK. YOU ARE A LION!'

Shuka, the parrot had been lost in his sleepy meditation. The sudden trumpeting of Muktak jerked him violently to wakefulness. That unhinged his brain, and he started screeching, 'LION! YOU ARE A LION!'

Muktak sighed deep at the cowardice of Sheru. 'We all had seen it coming. We tried, but we failed. A lion running away from the battlefield! What a shame!'

He then took a deep breath, turned around to face the wolf army, and walked slowly towards them.

'A minute, please.' Kurma appeared magically on the scene, and addressed Muktak.

'Nice to see you at this critical time of our existence,' Muktak sighed.

'Do not lose your heart for Sheru,' Kurma said. 'He is a lion who does not want to know that he is a lion. This is not happening for the first time. Nor will this be the last.'

'My world seems to have crashed around me. So many ifs and buts are crowding my head.'

'Why so? Why do you feel bad? You discharged your duties perfectly, and you worked sincerely. Then, why feel bad? The results of your actions are beyond your control. Why then feel bad about something over which you have no control? Brother, feel great because you worked greatly.'

Muktak knew that Kurma was right. Kurma was always right. Kurma – the master of universality – the master of what lies beyond individuality and collectivity.

Muktak sighed and said, 'Sir, now that Sheru is not here to protect our folks, allow me the leave to join the battle with the brutes.'

'Why call the attackers brutes? Only their hunger is different from your hunger. Be not personal about it.'

Kurma, the master, then jumped into the water body to float effortlessly towards the river to go back to his globetrotting.

'Best wishes, old Tusk!' It was Mr Python. He had hurried from his place of rest and was hanging from a tree to attract the attention of Muktak. 'I wish I could help you in your fight, but I have limits set by our code. We cannot interfere in the war of the leggies. Do not conclude from this that my wishes are not with you, my dear old wisdom!'

'Thank you, old survivor!'

Muktak now walked with determination towards the wolf army, and reached the open field that lay between him and the enemy. Initially, he stood firm and spread his ears to catch the faintest sound. He then started to sway backwards and forwards. His ears were now held back against the neck, and his trunk was tucked up against his chin – a sure sign of fight unto death.

Epilogue

The outcome of that great war is a different story, which may be narrated some other time.

However, there was one interesting outcome of the war that needs mention.

Shuka, the parrot, lost his head that day due to the sudden trumpeting of Muktak. From that time on, his mind kept going back to the refrain 'LION! YOU ARE A LION!'

Due to this, he continued screeching the words for the rest of his life. The forest lore is that he lost interest in everything else other than doing that.

The descendants of Shuka found the words to be so impressive that they too began to chant it like a mantra. It has now become the practice of the adult parrots to teach the younger ones the tradition of the words, which they consider sacred.

Even today, the parrots continue to screech those words. You can hear them shouting 'Lion! You are a lion!' while flying all over the world.

Most people do not pay attention to these screeches, and many find them annoying. After all, people have their own monkeys to carry on their backs, or have their own lettuce farms to tend.

When someone gets too annoyed by these screeches, he throws a stone at the annoying parrot, or shoos him away.

~∽∽~